# St. Irvyne; Or, The Rosicrucian

# St. Irvyne; Or, The Rosicrucian

**A Romance**

Percy Bysshe Shelley

MINT EDITIONS

*St. Irvyne; Or, The Rosicrucian: A Romance* was first published in 1810.

This edition published by Mint Editions 2021.

ISBN 9781513282718 | E-ISBN 9781513287737

Published by Mint Editions®

MINT
EDITIONS
minteditionbooks.com

Publishing Director: Jennifer Newens
Design & Production: Rachel Lopez Metzger
Project Manager: Micaela Clark
Typesetting: Westchester Publishing Services

# CONTENTS

# I

Red thunder-clouds, borne on the wings of the midnight whirlwind, floated, at fits, athwart the crimson-coloured orbit of the moon; the rising fierceness of the blast sighed through the stunted shrubs, which, bending before its violence, inclined towards the rocks whereon they grew: over the blackened expanse of heaven, at intervals, was spread the blue lightning's flash; it played upon the granite heights, and, with momentary brilliancy, disclosed the terrific scenery of the Alps, whose gigantic and mishapen summits, reddened by the transitory moon-beam, were crossed by black fleeting fragments of the tempest-clouds. The rain, in big drops, began to descend, and the thunder-peals, with louder and more deafening crash, to shake the zenith, till the long-protracted war, echoing from cavern to cavern, died, in indistinct murmurs, amidst the far-extended chain of mountains. In this scene, then, at this horrible and tempestuous hour, without one existent earthy being whom he might claim as friend, without one resource to which he might fly as an asylum from the horrors of neglect and poverty, stood Wolfstein;—he gazed upon the conflicting elements; his youthful figure reclined against a jutting granite rock; he cursed his wayward destiny, and implored the Almighty of Heaven to permit the thunderbolt, with crash terrific and exterminating, to descend upon his head, that a being useless to himself and to society might no longer, by his existence, mock Him whone'er made aught in vain. "And what so horrible crimes have I committed," exclaimed Wolfstein, driven to impiety by desperation, "what crimes which merit punishment like this? What, what is death?— Ah, dissolution! thy pang is blunted by the hard hand of long-protracted suffering—suffering unspeakable, indescribable!" As thus he spoke, a more terrific paroxysm of excessive despair revelled through every vein; his brain swam around in wild confusion, and, rendered delirious by excess of misery, he started from his flinty seat, and swiftly hastened towards the precipice, which yawned widely beneath his feet. "For what then should I longer drag on the galling chain of existence?" cried Wolfstein; and his impious expression was borne onwards by the hot and sulphurous thunder-blast.

The midnight meteors danced above the gulf upon which Wolfstein wistfully gazed. Palpable, impenetrable darkness seemed to hang upon it; impenetrable even by the flaming thunderbolt. "Into this then shall

I plunge myself?" soliloquized the wretched outcast, "and by one rash act endanger, perhaps, eternal happiness;—deliver myself up, perhaps, to the anticipation and experience of never-ending torments? Art thou the God then, the Creator of the universe, whom canting monks call the God of mercy and forgiveness, and sufferest thou thy creatures to become the victims of tortures such as fate has inflicted on me?—Oh! God, take my soul; why should I longer live?" Thus having spoken, he sank on the rocky bosom of the mountains. Yet, unheeding the exclamations of the maddened Wolfstein, fiercer raged the tempest. The battling elements, in wild confusion, seemed to threaten nature's dissolution; the ferocious thunderbolt, with impetuous violence, danced upon the mountains, and, collecting more terrific strength, severed gigantic rocks from their else eternal basements; the masses, with sound more frightful than the bursting thunder-peal, dashed towards the valley below. Horror and desolation marked their track. The mountain-rills, swoln by the waters of the sky, dashed with direr impetuosity from the Alpine summits; their foaming waters were hidden in the darkness of midnight, or only became visible when the momentary scintillations of the lightning rested on their whitened waves. Fiercer still than nature's wildest uproar were the feelings of Wolfstein's bosom; his frame, at last, conquered by the conflicting passions of his soul, no longer was adequate to sustain the unequal contest, but sank to the earth. His brain swam wildly, and he lay entranced in total insensibility.

What torches are those that dispel the distant darkness of midnight, and gleam, like meteors, athwart the blackness of the tempest? They throw a wavering light over the thickness of the storm: they wind along the mountains: they pass the hollow vallies. Hark! the howling of the blast has ceased,—the thunderbolts have dispersed, but yet reigns darkness. Distant sounds of song are borne on the breeze: the sounds approach. A low bier holds the remains of one whose soul is floating in the regions of eternity: a black pall covers him. Monks support the lifeless clay: others precede, bearing torches, and chanting a requiem for the salvation of the departed one. They hasten towards the convent of the valley, there to deposit the lifeless limbs of one who has explored the frightful path of eternity before them. And now they had arrived where lay Wolfstein: "Alas!" said one of the monks, "there reclines a wretched traveller. He is dead; murdered, doubtlessly, by the fell bandits who infest these wild recesses."

They raised from the earth his form: yet his bosom throbbed with the tide of life: returning animation once more illumed his eye: he started on his feet, and wildly inquired why they had awakened him from that slumber which he had hoped to have been eternal. Unconnected were his expressions, strange and impetuous the fire darting from his restless eyeballs. At length, the monks succeeded in calming the desperate tumultuousness of his bosom, calming at least in some degree; for he accepted their proffered tenders of a lodging, and essayed to lull to sleep, for a while, the horrible idea of dereliction which pressed upon his loaded brain.

While thus they stood, loud shouts rent the air, and, before Wolfstein and the monks could well collect their scattered faculties, they found that a troop of Alpine bandits had surrounded them. Trembling, from apprehension, the monks fled every way. None, however, could escape. "What! old greybeards," cried one of the robbers, "do you suppose that we will permit you to evade us: you who feed upon the strength of the country, in idleness and luxury, and have compelled many of our noble fellows, who otherwise would have been ornaments to their country in peace, thunderbolts to their enemies in war, to seek precarious subsistence as Alpine bandits? If you wish for mercy, therefore, deliver unhesitatingly your joint riches." The robbers then despoiled the monks of whatever they might adventitiously have taken with them, and, turning to Wolfstein, the apparent chieftain told him to yield his money likewise. Unappalled, Wolfstein advanced towards him. The chief held a torch; its red beams disclosed the expression of stern severity and unyielding loftiness which sate upon the brow of Wolfstein. "Bandit!" he answered fearlessly, "I have none,—no money—no hope— no friends; nor do I care for existence! Now judge if such a man be a fit victim for fear! No! I never trembled!"

A ray of pleasure gleamed in the countenance of the bandit as Wolfstein spoke. Grief, in inerasible traces, sate deeply implanted on the front of the outcast. At last, the chief, advancing to Wolfstein, who stood at some little distance, said, "My companions think that so noble a fellow as you appear to be, would be no unworthy member of our society; and, by Heaven, I am of their opinion. Are you willing to become one of us?"

Wolfstein's dark gaze was fixed upon the grounds his contracted eyebrow evinced deep thought: he started from his reverie, and, without hesitation, consented to their proposal.

Long was it past the hour of midnight when the banditti troop, with their newly-acquired associate, advanced along the pathless Alps. The red glare of the torches which each held, tinged the rocks and pine-trees, through woods of which they occasionally passed, and alone dissipated the darkness of night. Now had they arrived at the summit of a wild and rocky precipice, but the base indeed of another which mingled its far-seen and gigantic outline with the clouds of heaven. A door, which before had appeared part of the solid rock, flew open at the chieftain's touch, and the whole party advanced into the spacious cavern. Over the walls of the lengthened passages putrefaction had spread a bluish clamminess; damps hung around, and, at intervals, almost extinguished the torches, whose glare was scarcely sufficient to dissipate the impenetrable obscurity. After many devious windings they advanced into the body of the cavern: it was spacious and lofty. A blazing wood fire threw its dubious rays upon the mishapen and ill-carved walls. Lamps suspended from the roof, dispersed the subterranean gloom, not so completely however, but that ill-defined shades lurked in the arched distances, whose hollow recesses led to different apartments.

The gang had sate down in the midst of the cavern to supper, which a female, whose former loveliness had left scarce any traces on her cheek, had prepared. The most exquisite and expensive wines apologized for the rusticity of the rest of the entertainment, and induced freedom of conversation, and wild boisterous merriment, which reigned until the bandits, overcome by the fumes of the wine which they had drank, sank to sleep. Wolfstein, left again to solitude and silence, reclining on his mat in a corner of the cavern, retraced, in mental, sorrowing review, the past events of his life: ah! that eventful existence whose fate had dragged the heir of a wealthy potentate in Germany from the lap of luxury and indulgence, to become a vile associate of viler bandits, in the wild and trackless deserts of the Alps. Around their dwelling, lofty inaccessible acclivities reared their barren summits; they echoed to no sound save the wild hoot of the night-raven, or the impatient yelling of the vulture, which hovered on the blast in quest of scanty sustenance. These were the scenes without: noisy revelry and tumultuous riot reigned within. The mirth of the bandits appeared to arise independently of themselves: their hearts were void and dreary. Wolfstein's limbs pillowed on the flinty bosom of the earth: those limbs which had been wont to recline on the softest, the most luxurious sofas. Driven from his native country by an event which imposed upon him an insuperable barrier to ever again returning thither, possessing no friends, not having one single resource from which he might obtain support, where could the wretch, the exile, seek for an asylum but with those whose fortunes, expectations, and characters were desperate, and marked as darkly, by fate, as his own?

Time fled, and each succeeding day inured Wolfstein more and more to the idea of depriving his fellow-creatures of their possessions. In a short space of time the high-souled and noble Wolfstein, though still high-souled and noble, became an experienced bandit. His magnanimity and courage, even whilst surrounded by the most threatening dangers, and the unappalled expression of countenance with which he defied the dart of death, endeared him to the robbers: whilst with him they all asserted that they felt, as it were, instinctively impelled to deeds of horror and danger, which, otherwise, must have remained unattempted even by the boldest. His was every daring expedition, his the scheme which demanded depth of judgment and promptness of execution. Often, whilst at midnight the band lurked perhaps beneath the overhanging rocks, which were gloomily impended above them, in the midst, perhaps, of one of those horrible tempests whereby the air, in those Alpine regions, is so frequently convulsed, would the countenance of the bandits betray some slight shade of alarm and awe; but that of Wolfstein was fixed, unchanged, by any variation of scenery or action. One day it was when the chief communicated to the banditti, notice which he had received by means of spies, that an Italian Count of immense wealth was journeying from Paris to his native country, and, at a late hour the following evening, would pass the Alps near this place; "They have but few attendants," added he, "and those few will not come this way; the postillion is in our interest, and the horses are to be overcome with fatigue when they approach the destined spot: you understand."

The evening came. "I," said Wolfstein, "will roam into the country, but will return before the arrival of our wealthy victim." Thus saying, he left the cavern, and wandered out amidst the mountains.

It was autumn. The mountain-tops, the scattered oaks which occasionally waved their lightning-blasted heads on the summits of the far-seen piles of rock, were gilded by the setting glory of the sun; the trees, yellowed by the waning year, reflected a glowing teint from their thick foliage; and the dark pine-groves which were stretched half way up the mountain sides, added a more deepened gloom to the shades of evening, which already began to gather rapidly above the scenery.

It was at this dark and silent hour, that Wolfstein, unheeding the surrounding objects,—objects which might have touched with awe, or heightened to devotion, any other breast,—wandered alone—pensively he wandered—dark images for futurity possessed his soul: he shuddered when he reflected upon what had passed; nor was his present situation calculated to satisfy a mind eagerly panting for liberty and independence. Conscience too, awakened conscience, upbraided him for the life which he had selected, and, with silent whisperings, stung his soul to madness. Oppressed by thoughts such as these, Wolfstein yet proceeded, forgetful that he was to return before the arrival of their destined victim—forgetful indeed was he of every external existence; and absorbed in himself, with arms folded, and eyes fixed upon the earth, he yet advanced. At last he sank on a mossy bank, and, guided by the impulse of the moment, inscribed on a tablet the following lines; for the inaccuracy of which, the perturbation of him who wrote them, may account; he thought of past times while he marked the paper with—

"'T was dead of the night, when I sat in my dwelling;
One glimmering lamp was expiring and low;
Around, the dark tide of the tempest was swelling.
Along the wild mountains night-ravens were yelling,—
They bodingly presag'd destruction and woe.
'T was then that I started!—the wild storm was howling.
Nought was seen, save the lightning, which danc'd in the sky;
Above me, the crash of the thunder was rolling.
And low, chilling murmurs, the blast wafted by.
My heart sank within me—unheeded the war
Of the battling clouds, on the mountain-tops, broke;—
Unheeded the thunder-peal crash'd in mine ear—
This heart, hard as iron, is stranger to fear;
But conscience in low, noiseless whispering spoke.
'T was then that her form on the whirlwind upholding.
The ghost of the murder'd Victoria strode;
In her right hand, a shadowy shroud she was holding.
She swiftly advanc'd to my lonesome abode.
I wildly then call'd on the tempest to bear me—"

Overcome by the wild retrospection of ideal horror, which these swiftly-written lines excited in his soul, Wolfstein tore the paper, on which he had written them, to pieces, and scattered them about him. He arose from his recumbent posture, and again advanced through the forest. Not far had he proceeded, ere a mingled murmur broke upon the silence of night—it was the sound of human voices. An event so unusual in these solitudes, excited Wolfstein's momentary surprise; he started, and looking around him, essayed to discover whence those sounds proceeded.—What was the astonishment of Wolfstein, when he found that a detached party, who had been sent in pursuit of the Count, had actually overtaken him, and, at this instant, were dragging from the carriage the almost lifeless form of a female, whose light symmetrical figure, as it leant on the muscular frame of the robber who supported it, afforded a most striking contrast.—They had, before his arrival, plundered the Count of all his riches, and, enraged at the spirited defence which he had made, had inhumanly murdered him, and cast his lifeless body adown the yawning precipice. Transfixed by a jutting point of granite rock, it remained there to be devoured by the ravens. Wolfstein joined the banditti: and, although he could not recall the deed, lamented the wanton cruelty which had been practised upon the Count. As for the female, whose grace and loveliness made so strong an impression upon him, he demanded that every soothing attention should be paid to her, and his desire was enforced by the commands of the chief, whose dark eye wandered wildly over the beauties of the lovely Megalena de Metastasio, as if he had secretly destined them for himself.

At last they arrived at the cavern; every resource which the cavern of a gang of lawless and desperate villains might afford, was brought forward to restore the fainted Megalena to life: she soon recovered— she slowly opened her eyes, and started with surprise to behold herself surrounded by a rough set of desperadoes, and the gloomy walls of the cavern, upon which darkness hung, awfully visible. Near her sate a female, whose darkened expression of countenance seemed perfectly to correspond with the horror prevalent throughout the cavern; her face, though bearing the marks of an undeniable expression of familiarity with wretchedness, had some slight remains of beauty.

It was long past midnight when each of the robbers withdrew to repose. But his mind was too much occupied by the events of the evening to allow the unhappy Wolfstein to find quiet;—at an early hour he arose from his sleepless couch, to inhale the morning breeze. The sun had but just risen; the scene was beautiful; every thing was still, and seemed to favour that reflection, which even propinquity to his abandoned associates imposed no indefinably insuperable bar to. In spite of his attempts to think upon other subjects, the image of the fair Megalena floated in his mind. Her loveliness had made too deep an impression on it to be easily removed; and the hapless Wolfstein, ever the victim of impulsive feeling, found himself bound to her by ties, more lasting than he had now conceived the transitory tyranny of woe could have imposed. For never had Wolfstein beheld so singularly beautiful a form;—her figure cast in the mould of most exact symmetry; her blue and love-beaming eyes, from which occasionally emanated a wild expression, seemingly almost superhuman; and the auburn hair which hung in unconfined tresses down her damask cheek—formed a resistless tout ensemble.

Heedless of every external object, Wolfstein long wandered.—The protracted sound of the bandits' horn struck at last upon his ear, and aroused him from his reverie. On his return to the cavern, the robbers were assembled at their meal; the chief regarded him with marked and jealous surprise as he entered, but made no remark. They then discussed their uninteresting and monotonous topics, and the meal being ended, each villain departed on his different business.

Megalena, finding herself alone with Agnes (the only woman, save herself, who was in the cavern, and who served as an attendant on the robbers), essayed, by the most humble entreaties and supplications, to excite pity in her breast: she conjured her to explain the cause for which she was thus imprisoned, and wildly inquired for her father. The guilt-bronzed brow of Agnes was contracted by a sullen and malicious frown: it was the only reply which the inhuman female deigned to return. After a pause, however, she said, "Thou thinkest thyself my superior, proud girl; but time may render us equals.—Submit to that, and you may live on the same terms as I do."

There appeared to lurk a meaning in these words, which Megalena found herself incompetent to develope; she answered not, therefore, and suffered Agnes to depart unquestioned. The wretched Megalena, a prey to despair and terror, endeavoured to revolve in her mind the events which had brought her to this spot, but an unconnected stream of ideas pressed upon her brain. The sole light in her cell was that of a dismal lamp, which, by its uncertain flickering, only dissipated the almost palpable obscurity, in a sufficient degree more assuredly to point out the circumambient horrors. She gazed wistfully around, to see if

PERCY BYSSHE SHELLEY

there were any outlet; none there was, save the door whereby Agnes had entered, which was strongly barred on the outside. In despair she threw herself on the wretched pallet.—"For what cause, then, am I thus entombed alive?" soliloquized the hapless Megalena; "would it not be preferable at once to annihilate the spark of life which burns but faintly within my bosom?—O my father! where art thou? Thy tombless corse, perhaps, is torn into a thousand pieces by the fury of the mountain cataract.—Little didst thou presage misfortunes such as these!—little didst thou suppose that our last journey would have caused thy immature dissolution—my infamy and misery, not to end but with my hapless existence!—Here there is none to comfort me, none to participate my miseries!" Thus speaking, overcome by a paroxysm of emotion, she sank on the bed, and bedewed her fair face with tears.

Whilst, oppressed by painful retrospection, the outcast orphan was yet kneeling, Agnes entered, and, not even noticing her distress, bade her prepare to come to the banquet where the troop of bandits was assembled. In silence, along the vaulted and gloomy passages, she followed her conductress, from whose stern and forbidding gaze her nature shrunk back enhorrored, till they reached that apartment of the cavern where the revelry waited but for her arrival to commence. On her entering, Cavigni, the chief, led her to a seat on his right hand, and paid her every attention which his froward nature could stoop to exercise towards a female: she received his civilities with apparent complacency; but her eye was frequently fascinated, as it were, towards the youthful Wolfstein, who had caught her attention the evening before. His countenance, spite of the shade of woe with which the hard hand of suffering had marked it, was engaging and beautiful; not that beauty which may be freely acknowledged, but inwardly confessed by every beholder with sensations penetrating and resistless; his figure majestic and lofty, and the fire which flashed from his expressive eye, indefinably to herself, penetrated the inmost soul of the isolated Megalena. Wolfstein regarded Cavigni with indignation and envy; and, though almost ignorant himself of the dreadful purpose of his soul, resolved in his own mind an horrible deed. Cavigni was enraptured with the beauty of Megalena, and secretly vowed that no paius should be spared to gain to himself the possession of an object so lovely. The anticipated delight of gratified voluptuousness revelled in every vein, as he gazed upon her; his eye flashed with a triumphant expression of lawless love, yet he determined to defer the hour of his happiness till he might enjoy more free, unrestrained delight, with his adored fair one. She gazed on the chief, however, with an ill-concealed aversion; his dark expression of countenance, the haughty severity, and contemptuous frown, which habitually sate on his brow, invited not, but rather repelled a reciprocality of affection, which the haughty chief, after his own attachment, entertained not the most distant doubt of. He was, notwithstanding, conscious of her coldness, but attributing it to virgin modesty, or to the novel situation into which she had suddenly been thrown, paid her every attention; nor did he omit to promise her every little comfort which might induce her to regard him with esteem. Still, though veiled beneath the most artful dissimulation, did the fair Megalena pant ardently for liberty—for, oh! liberty is sweet, sweeter even than all the other pleasures of life, to full satiety, without it.

Cavigni essayed, by every art, to gain her over to his desires; but Megalena, regarding him with aversion, answered with an haughtiness which she was unable to conceal, and which his proud spirit might ill brook. Cavigni could not disguise the vexation which he felt, when, increased by resistance, Megalena's dislike towards him remained no longer a secret: "Megalena," said he, at last, "fair girl, thou shalt be mine—we will be wedded tomorrow, if you think the bands of love not sufficiently forcible to unite us."

"No bands shall ever unite me to you!" exclaimed Megalena. "Even though the grave were to yawn beneath my feet, I would willingly precipitate myself into its gulf, if the alternative of that, or an union with you, were proposed to me."

Rage swelled Cavigni's bosom almost to bursting—the conflicting passions of his soul were too tumultuous for utterance;—in an hurried tone, he commanded Agnes to show Megalena to her cell: she obeyed, and they both quitted the apartment.

Wolfstein's soul, sublimed by the most infuriate paroxysms of contending emotions, battled wildly. His countenance retained, however, but one expression,—it was of dark and deliberate revenge. His stern eye was fixed upon Cavigni;—he decided at this instant to perpetrate the deed he had resolved on. Leaving his seat, he intimated his intention of quitting the cavern for an instant.

Cavigni had just filled his goblet—Wolfstein, as he passed, dexterously threw a little white powder into the wine of the chief.

When Wolfstein returned, Cavigni had not yet quaffed the deadly draught: rising, therefore, he exclaimed aloud, "Fill your goblets, all."

Every one obeyed, and sat in expectation of the toast which he was about to propose.

"Let us drink," he exclaimed, "to the health of the chieftain's bride—let us drink to their mutual happiness." A smile of pleasure irradiated the countenance of the chief:—that he whom he had supposed to be a dangerous rival, should thus publicly forego any claim to the affections of Megalena, was indeed pleasure.

"Health and mutual happiness to the chieftain and his bride!" re-echoed from every part of the table.

Cavigni raised the goblet to his lips: he was about to quaff the tide of death, when Ginotti, one of the robbers, who sat next to him, upreared his arm, and dashed the cup of destruction to the earth. A silence, as if in expectation of some terrible event, reigned throughout the cavern.

Wolfstein turned his eyes towards the chief;—the dark and mysterious gaze of Ginotti arrested his wandering eyeball; its expression was too marked to be misunderstood;—he trembled in his inmost soul, but his countenance yet retained its unchangeable expression. Ginotti spoke not, nor willed he to assign any reason for his extraordinary conduct; the circumstance was shortly forgotten, and the revelry went on undisturbed by any other event.

Ginotti was one of the boldest of the robbers; he was the distinguished favourite of the chief, and, although mysterious and reserved, his society was courted with more eagerness, than such qualities might, abstractedly considered, appear to deserve. None knew his history—that he concealed within the deepest recesses of his bosom; nor could the most suppliant entreaties, or threats of the most horrible punishments, have wrested from him one particular concerning it. Never had he once thrown off the mysterious mask, beneath which his character was veiled, since he had become an associate of the band. In vain the chief required him to assign some reason for his late extravagant conduct; he said it was mere accident, but with an air, which more than convinced every one, that something lurked behind which yet remained unknown. Such, however, was their respect for Ginotti, that the occurrence passed almost without a comment.

Long now had the hour of midnight gone by, and the bandits had retired to repose. Wolfstein retired too to his couch, but sleep closed not his eyelids; his bosom was a scene of the wildest anarchy; the conflicting passions revelled dreadfully in his burning brain:—love, maddening, excessive, unaccountable idolatry, as it were, which possessed him for

Megalena, urged him on to the commission of deeds which conscience represented as beyond measure wicked, and which Ginotti's glance convinced him were by no means unsuspected. Still so unbounded was his love for Megalena (madness rather than love), that it overbalanced every other consideration, and his unappalled soul resolved to persevere in its determination even to destruction!

Cavigni's commands respecting Megalena had been obeyed:—the door of her cell was fastened, and the ferocious chief resolved to let her lie there till the suffering and confinement might subdue her to his will. Megalena endeavoured, by every means, to soften the obdurate heart of her attendant; at length, her mildness of manner induced Agnes to regard her with pity; and before she quitted the cell, they were so far reconciled to each other, that they entered into a comparison of their mutual situations; and Agnes was about to relate to Megalena the circumstances which had brought her to the cavern, when the fierce Cavigni entered, and, commanding Agnes to withdraw, said, "Well, proud girl, are you now in a better humour to return the favour with which your superior regards you?"

"No!" heroically answered Megalena.

"Then," rejoined the chief, "if within four-and-twenty hours you hold yourself not in readiness to return my love, force shall wrest the jewel from its casket." Thus having said, he abruptly quitted the cell.

So far had Wolfstein's proposed toast, at the banquet, gained on the unsuspecting ferociousness of Cavigni, that he accepted the former's artful tender of service, in the way of persuasion with Megalena, supposing, by Wolfstein's manner, that they had been cursorily acquainted before. Wolfstein, therefore, entered the apartment of Megalena.

At the sight of him Megalena arose from her recumbent posture, and hastened joyfully to meet him; for she remembered that Wolfstein had rescued her from the insults of the banditti, on the eventful evening which had subjected her to their control.

"Lovely, adored girl," he exclaimed, "short is my time: pardon, therefore, the abruptness of my address. The chief has sent me to persuade you to become united to him; but I love you, I adore you to madness. I am not what I seem. Answer me!—time is short."

An indefinable sensation, unfelt before, swelled through the passion-quivering frame of Megalena. "Yes, yes," she cried, "I will—I love you—" At this instant the voice of Cavigni was heard in the passage. Wolfstein started from his knees, and pressing the fair hand presented to his lips with exulting ardour, departed hastily to give an account of his mission to the anxious Cavigni; who restrained himself in the passage without, and, slightly mistrusting Wolfstein, was about to advance to the door of the cell to listen to their conversation, when Wolfstein quitted Megalena.

Megalena, again in solitude, began to reflect upon the scenes which had been lately acted. She thought upon the words of Wolfstein, unconscious wherefore they were a balm to her mind: she reclined upon her wretched pallet. It was now night: her thoughts took a different turn; the melancholy wind sighing along the crevices of the cavern, and the dismal sound of rain which pattered fast, inspired mournful reflection. She thought of her father,—her beloved father;—a solitary wanderer on the face of the earth; or, most probably, thought she, his soul rests in death. Horrible idea If the latter, she envied his fate; if the former, she even supposed it preferable to her present abode. She again thought of Wolfstein; she pondered on his last words:—an escape from the cavern: oh delightful idea! Again her thoughts recurred to her father: tears bedewed her cheeks; she took a pencil, and, actuated by the feelings of the moment, inscribed on the wall of her prison these lines:

> *Ghosts of the dead! have I not heard your yelling*
> *Rise on the night-rolling breath of the blast.*
> *When o'er the dark ether the tempest is swelling.*
> *And on eddying whirlwind the thunder-peal past?*
> *For oft have I stood on the dark height of Jura.*
> *Which frowns on the valley that opens beneath;*
> *Oft have I brav'd the chill night-tempest's fury.*
> *Whilst around me, I thought, echo'd murmurs of death.*
> *And now, whilst the winds of the mountain are howling.*
> *O father! thy voice seems to strike on mine ear;*
> *In air whilst the tide of the night-storm is rolling.*
> *It breaks on the pause of the elements' jar.*
> *On the wing of the whirlwind which roars o'er the mountain*
> *Perhaps rides the ghost of my sire who is dead;*
> *On the mist of the tempest which hangs o'er the fountain.*

Whilst a wreath of dark vapour encircles his head. Here she paused, and, ashamed of the exuberance of her imagination, obliterated from the wall the characters which she had traced: the wind still howled dreadfully: in fearful anticipation of the morrow, she threw herself on the bed, and, in sleep, forgot the misfortunes which impended over her.

Meantime, the soul of Wolfstein was disturbed by ten thousand conflicting passions; revenge and disappointed love agonized his soul to madness; and he resolved to quench the rude feelings of his bosom in the blood of his rival. But, again he thought of Ginotti; he thought of the mysterious intervention which his dark glances proved not to be accidental. To him it was an inexplicable mystery; which the more he reflected upon, the less able was he to unravel. He had mixed the poison, unseen, as he thought, by any one; certainly unseen by Ginotti, whose back was unconcernedly turned at the time. He planned, therefore, a second attempt, unawed by what had happened before, for the destruction of Cavigni, which he resolved to put into execution this night.

Before he had become an associate with the band of robbers, the conscience of Wolfstein was clear; clear, at least, from the commission of any wilful and deliberate crime: for, alas! an event almost too dreadful for narration, had compelled him to quit his native country, in indigence and disgrace. His courage was equal to his wickedness; his mind was unalienable from its purpose; and whatever his will might determine, his boldness would fearlessly execute, even though hell and destruction were to yawn beneath his feet, and essay to turn his unappalled soul from the accomplishment of his design. Such was the guilty Wolfstein; a disgraceful fugitive from his country, a vile associate of a band of robbers, and a murderer, at least in intent, if not in deed. He shrunk not at the commission of crimes; he was now the hardened villain; eternal damnation, tortures inconceivable on earth, awaited him. "Foolish, degrading idea!" he exclaimed, as it momentarily glanced through his mind; "am I worthy of the celestial Megalena, if I shrink at the price which it is necessary I should pay for her possession?" This idea banished every other feeling from his heart; and, smothering the stings of conscience, a decided resolve of murder took possession of him—the determining, within himself, to destroy the very man who had given him an asylum, when driven to madness by the horrors of neglect and poverty. He stood in the night-storm on the mountains; he cursed the intervention of Ginotti, and secretly swore that nor heaven nor hell again should dash the goblet of destruction from the mouth of the detested Cavigni. The soul of Wolfstein too, insatiable in its desires, and panting for liberty, ill could brook the confinement of idea, which the cavern of the bandits must necessarily induce. He longed again to try his fortune; he longed to re-enter that world which he had never tried but once, and that indeed for a short time; sufficiently long, however, to blast his blooming hopes, and to graft on the stock, which otherwise might have produeed virtue, the fatal seeds of vice.

# II

The fiends of fate are heard to rave.
And the death-angel flaps his broad wing o'er the wave.

It was midnight; and all the robbers were assembled in the banquet-hall, amongst whom, bearing in his bosom a weight of premeditated crime, was Wolfstein; he sat by the chief. They discoursed on indifferent subjects; the sparkling goblet went round; loud laughter succeeded. The ruffians were rejoicing over some plunder which they had taken from a traveller, whom they had robbed of immense wealth; they had left his body a prey to the vultures of the mountains. The table groaned with the pressure of the feast. Hilarity reigned around: reiterated were the shouts of merriment and joy; if such could exist in a cavern of robbers.

It was long past midnight: another hour, and Megalena must be Cavigni's. This idea rendered Wolfstein callous to every sting of conscience; and he eagerly awaited an opportunity when he might, unperceived, infuse poison into the goblet of one who confided in him. Ginotti sat opposite to Wolfstein: his arms were folded, and his gaze rested fixedly upon the fearless countenance of the murderer. Wolfstein shuddered when he beheld the brow of the mysterious Ginotti contracted, his marked features wrapped in inexplicable mystery.

All were now heated by wine, save the wily villain who destined murder; and the awe-inspiring Ginotti, whose reservedness and mystery, not even the hilarity of the present hour could dispel.

Conversation appearing to flag, Cavigni exclaimed, "Steindolph, you know some old German stories; cannot you tell one, to deceive the lagging hours?"

Steindolph was famed for his knowledge of metrical spectre tales, and the gang were frequently wont to hang delighted on the ghostly wonders which he related.

"Excuse, then, the mode of my telling it," said Steindolph, "and I will with pleasure. I learnt it whilst in Germany; my old grandmother taught it me, and I can repeat it as a ballad."—"Do, do," re-echoed from every part of the cavern.—Steindolph thus began:

# BALLAD

## I

The death-bell beats!—
The mountain repeats
The echoing sound of the knell;
And the dark monk now
Wraps the cowl round his brow.
As he sits in his lonely cell.

## II

And the cold hand of death
Chills his shuddering breath.
As he lists to the fearful lay
Which the ghosts of the sky.
As they sweep wildly by.
Sing to departed day.
And they sing of the hour
When the stern fates had power
To resolve Rosa's form to its clay.

## III

But that hour is past;
And that hour was the last
Of peace to the dark monk's brain.
Bitter tears, from his eyes, gush'd silent and fast;
And he strove to suppress them in vain.

## IV

Then his fair cross of gold he dash'd on the floor.
When the death-knell struck on his ear. Delight is in store
For her evermore;
But for me is fate, horror, and fear.

## V

*Then his eyes wildly roll'd.*
*When the death-bell toll'd.*
*And he rag'd in terrific woe.*
*And he stamp'd on the ground,—*
*But when ceas'd the sound.*
*Tears again began to flow.*

## VI

*And the ice of despair*
*Chill'd the wild throb of care.*
*And he sate in mute agony still;*
*Till the night-stars shone through the cloudless air.*
*And the pale moon-beam slept on the hill.*

## VII

*Then he knelt in his cell:—*
*And the horrors of hell*
*Were delights to his agoniz'd pain.*
*And he pray'd to God to dissolve the spell.*
*Which else must for ever remain.*

## VIII

*And in fervent pray'r he knelt on the ground.*
*Till the abbey bell struck One:*
*His feverish blood ran chill at the sound:*
*A voice hollow and horrible murmur'd around—*
*"The term of thy penance is done!"*

## IX

*Grew dark the night;*
*The moon-beam bright*
*Wax'd faint on the mountain high;*
*And, from the black hill.*

Went a voice cold and still,—
"Monk! thou art free to die."

## X

Then he rose on his feet.
And his heart loud did beat.
And his limbs they were palsied with dread;
Whilst the grave's clammy dew
O'er his pale forehead grew;
And he shudder'd to sleep with the dead.

## XI

And the wild midnight storm
Rav'd around his tall form.
As he sought the chapel's gloom:
And the sunk grass did sigh
To the wind, bleak and high.
As he search'd for the new-made tomb.

## XII

And forms, dark and high.
Seem'd around him to fly.
And mingle their yells with the blast:
And on the dark wall
Half-seen shadows did fall.
As enhorror'd he onward pass'd.

## XIII

And the storm-fiend's wild rave
O'er the new-made grave.
And dread shadows, linger around.
The Monk call'd on God his soul to save.
And, in horror, sank on the ground.

## XIV

Then despair nerv'd his arm
To dispel the charm.
And he burst Rosa's coffin asunder.
And the fierce storm did swell
More terrific and fell.
And louder peal'd the thunder.

## XV

And laugh'd, in joy, the fiendish throng.
Mix'd with ghosts of the mouldering dead:
And their grisly wings, as they floated along.
Whistled in murmurs dread.

## XVI

And her skeleton form the dead Nun rear'd.
Which dripp'd with the chill dew of hell.
In her half-eaten eyeballs two pale flames appear'd.
And triumphant their gleam on the dark Monk glar'd.
As he stood within the cell.

## XVII

And her lank hand lay on his shuddering brain;
But each power was nerv'd by fear.—
"I never, henceforth, may breathe again;
Death now ends mine anguish'd pain.—
The grave yawns,—we meet there."

## XVIII

And her skeleton lungs did utter the sound.
So deadly, so lone, and so fell.
That in long vibrations shudder'd the ground;
And as the stern notes floated around.
A deep groan was answer'd from hell.

As Steindolph concluded, an universal shout of applause echoed through the cavern. Every one had been so attentive to the recitation of the robber, that no opportunity of perpetrating his resolve had appeared to Wolfstein. Now all again was revelry and riot, and the wily designer eagerly watched for the instant when universal confusion might favour his attempt to drop, unobserved, the powder into the goblet of the chief. With a gaze of insidious and malignant revenge was the eye of Wolfstein fixed upon the chieftain's countenance. Cavigni perceived it not; for he was heated with wine, or the unusual expression of his associate's face must have awakened suspicion, or excited remark. Yet was Ginotti's gaze fixed upon Wolfstein, who, like a sanguinary and remorseless ruffian, sat expectantly waiting the instant of death. The goblet passed round:—at the moment when Wolfstein mingled the poison with Cavigni's wine, the eyes of Ginotti, which before had regarded him with the most dazzling scrutiny, were intentionally turned away: he then arose from the table, and, complaining of sudden indisposition, retired. Cavigni raised the goblet to his lips—

"Now, my brave fellows," he exclaimed, "the hour is late; but before we retire, I here drink success and health to every one of you."

Wolfstein involuntarily shuddered.—Cavigni quaffed the liquor to the dregs!—the cup fell from his trembling hand. The chill dew of death sat upon his forehead: in terrific convulsion he fell headlong; and, inarticulately uttering "I am poisoned," sank seemingly lifeless on the earth. Sixty robbers at once rushed forward to raise him; and, reclining in their arms, with an horrible and harrowing shriek, the spark of life fled from his body for ever. A robber, skilled in surgery, opened a vein; but no blood followed the touch of the lancet.—Wolfstein advanced to the body, unappalled by the crime which he had committed, and tore aside the vest from its bosom: that bosom was discoloured by large spots of livid purple, which, by their premature appearance, declared the poison which had been used to destroy him, to be excessively powerful.

Every one regretted the death of the brave Cavigni; every one was surprised at the mode of his death: and, by his abruptly quitting the apartment, the suspicion fell upon Ginotti, who was consequently sent for by Ardolph, a robber whom they had chosen chieftain, Wolfstein having declined the proffered distinction.

Ginotti arrived.—His stern countenance was changed not by the execrations showered on him by every one. He yet remained unmoved, and apparently careless what sentiments others might entertain of him:

he deigned not even to deny the charge. This coolness seemed to have convinced every one, the new chief in particular, of his innocence.

"Let every one," said Ardolph, "be searched; and if his pockets contain poison which could have effected this, let him die." This method was universally applauded. As soon as the acclamations were stilled, Wolfstein advanced forwards, and spoke thus:

"Any longer to conceal that it was I who perpetrated the deed, were useless. Megalena's loveliness inflamed me:—I envied one who was about to possess it.—I have murdered him!"

Here he was interrupted by the shouts of the bandits; and he was about to be delivered to death, when Ginotti advanced. His superior and towering figure inspired awe even in the hearts of the bandits. They were silent.

"Suffer Wolfstein," he exclaimed, "to depart unhurt. I will answer for his never publishing our retreat: I will promise that never more shall you behold him."

Every one submitted to Ginotti: for who could resist the superior Ginotti? From the gaze of Ginotti Wolfstein's soul shrank, enhorrored, in confessed inferiority: he who had shrunk not at death, had shrunk not to avow himself guilty of murder, and had prepared to meet its reward, started from Ginotti's eye-beam as from the emanation of some superior and preter-human being.

"Quit the cavern!" said Ginotti.—"May I not remain here until the morrow?" inquired Wolfstein.—"If tomorrow's rising sun finds you in this cavern," returned Ginotti, "I must deliver you up to the vengeance of those whom you have injured."

Wolfstein retired to his solitary cell, to retrace, in his mind, the occurrences of this eventful night. What was he now?—an isolated wicked wanderer; not a being on earth whom he could call a friend, and carrying with him that never-dying tormentor—conscience. In half-waking dreams passed the night: the ghost of him whom he had so inhumanly destroyed, seemed to cry for justice at the throne of God; bleeding, pale, and ghastly, it pressed on his agonized brain; and confused, inexplicable visions flitted in his imagination, until the freshness of the morning breeze warned him to depart. He collected together all those valuables which had fallen to his share as plunder, during his stay in the cavern: they amounted to a large sum. He rushed from the cavern; he hesitated,—he knew not whither to fly. He walked fast, and essayed, by exercise, to smother the feelings of his soul; but the attempt was fruitless. Not far had he proceeded, ere, stretched on the earth apparently lifeless, he beheld a female form. He advanced towards it—it was Megalena!

A tumult of exulting and inconceivable transport rushed through his veins as he beheld her—her for whom he had plunged into the abyss of crime. She slept, and, apparently overcome by the fatigues which she had sustained, her slumber was profound. Her head reclined upon the jutting root of a tree: the tint of health and loveliness sat upon her cheek.

When the fair Megalena awakened, and found herself in the arms of Wolfstein, she started; yet, turning her eyes, she beheld it was no enemy, and the expression of terror gave way to pleasure. In the general confusion had Megalena escaped from the abode of the bandits. The destinies of Wolfstein and Megalena were assimilated by similarity of situations; and, before they quitted the spot, so far had this reciprocal feeling prevailed, that they swore mutual affection. Megalena then related her escape from the cavern, and showed Wolfstein jewels, to an immense amount, which she had secreted.

"At all events, then," said Wolfstein, "we may defy poverty; for I have about me jewels to the value of ten thousand zechins."

"We will go to Genoa," said Megalena. "We will, my fair one. There, entirely devoted to each other, we will defy the darts of misery."

Megalena returned no answer, save a look of else inexpressible love.

It was now the middle of the day; neither Wolfstein nor Megalena had tasted food since the preceding night; and faint, from fatigue, Megalena scarce could move onwards. "Courage, my love," said Wolfstein; "yet a little way, and we shall arrive at a cottage, a sort of inn, where we may wait until the morrow, and hire mules to carry us to Placenza, whence we can easily proceed to the goal of our destination."

Megalena collected her strength: in a short time they arrived at the cottage, and passed the remainder of the day in plans respecting the future. Wearied with unusual exertions, Megalena early retired to an inconvenient bed, which, however, was the best the cottage could afford; and Wolfstein, lying along the bench by the fireplace, resigned himself to meditation; for his mind was too much disturbed to let him sleep.

Although Wolfstein had every reason to rejoice at the success which had crowned his schemes; although the very event had occurred which his soul had so much and so eagerly panted for; yet, even now, in possession of all he held valuable on earth, was he ill at ease. Remorse for his crimes, tortured him: yet, steeling his conscience, he essayed to smother the fire which burned within his bosom; to change the tenour of his thoughts—in vain! he could not. Restless passed the night, and the middle of the day beheld Wolfstein and Megalena far from the habitation of the bandits.

They intended, if possible, to reach Breno that night, and thence, on the following day, to journey towards Genoa. They had descended the southern acclivity of the Alps. It was now hastening towards spring, and the whole country began to gleam with the renewed loveliness of nature. Odoriferous orange-groves scented the air. Myrtles bloomed on the sides of the gentle eminences which they occasionally ascended. The face of nature was smiling and gay; so was Megalena's heart: with exulting and speechless transport it bounded within her bosom. She gazed on him who possessed her soul; although she felt no inclination in her bosom to retrace the events, by means of which an obscure bandit, undefinable to herself, had gained the eternal love of the former haughty Megalena di Metastasio.

They soon arrived at Breno. Wolfstein dismissed the muleteer, and conducted Megalena into the interior of the inn, ordering at the same time a supper. Again were repeated protestations of eternal affection, avowals of indissoluble love; but it is sufficient to conceive what cannot be so well described.

It was near midnight; Wolfstein and Megalena sat at supper, and conversed with that unrestrainedness and gaiety which mutual confidence inspired, when the door was opened, and the innkeeper announced the arrival of a man who wished to speak with Wolfstein.

"Tell him," exclaimed Wolfstein, rather surprised, and wishing to guard against the possibility of danger, "that I will not see him."

The landlord left the room, and, in a short time, returned. A man accompanied him: he was of gigantic stature, and masked. "He would take no denial, Signor," said the landlord, in exculpation, as he left the room.

The stranger advanced to the table at which Wolfstein and Megalena sat: he threw aside his mask, and disclosed the features of—Ginotti! Wolfstein's frame became convulsed with involuntary horror: he started. Megalena was surprised.

Ginotti, at length, broke the terrible silence.

"Wolfstein," he said, "I saved you from, otherwise, inevitable death;

by my means alone have you gained Megalena:—what do I then deserve in return?" Wolfstein looked on the countenance: it was stern and severe, yet divested of the terrible expression which had before caused his frame to shudder with excess of alarm.

"My eternal gratitude," returned Wolfstein, hesitatingly.

"Will you promise, that when, destitute and a wanderer, I demand your protection, when I beseech you to listen to the tale which I shall relate, you will listen to me; that, when I am dead, you will bury me, and suffer my soul to rest in the endless slumber of annihilation? Then will you repay me for the benefits which I have conferred upon you."

"I will," replied Wolfstein, "I will perform all that you require."

"Swear it!" exclaimed Ginotti.

"I swear."

Ginotti then abruptly quitted the apartment; the sound of his footsteps was heard descending the stairs; and, when they were no longer audible, a weight seemed to have been taken from the breast of Wolfstein.

"How did that man save your life?" inquired Megalena.

"He was one of our band," replied Wolfstein, evasively, "and, on a plundering excursion, his pistol-ball entered the heart of the man, whose sabre, lifted aloft, would else have severed my head from my body."

"Dear Wolfstein, who are you?—whence came you?—for you were not always an Alpine bandit?"

"That is true, my adored one; but fate presents an insuperable barrier to my ever relating the events which occurred previously to my connexion with the banditti. Dearest Megalena, if you love me, never question me concerning my past life, but rest satisfied with the conviction, that my future existence shall be devoted to you, and to you alone." Megalena felt surprise; but although eagerly desiring to unravel the mystery in which Wolfstein shrouded himself, desisted from inquiry.

Ginotti's mysterious visit had made too serious an impression on the mind of Wolfstein to be lightly erased. In vain he essayed to appear easy and unembarrassed while he conversed with Megalena. He attempted to drown thought in wine—but in vain:—Ginotti's strange injunction pressed, like a load of ice, upon his breast. At last, the hour being late, they both retired to their respective rooms.

Early on the following morning, Wolfstein arose, to arrange the necessary preparations for their journey to Genoa; whither he had sent a servant whom he hired at Breno, to prepare accommodations for their arrival.—Needless were it minutely to describe each trivial event which occurred during their journey to Genoa.

On the morning of the fourth day, they found themselves within a short distance of the city. They determined on the plan which they should adopt, and, in a short space of time, arriving at Genoa, took up their residence in a mansion on the outermost extremity of the city.

# III

*Whence, and what art thou, execrable shape.*
*That dar'st, though grim and terrible, advance*
*Thy miscreated front athwart my way?*

—Paradise Lost

Time passed; and, settled in their new habitation, Megalena and Wolfstein appeared to defy the arrows of vengeful destiny.

Wolfstein resolved to allow some time to elapse before he spoke of the subject nearest to his heart, of herself, to Megalena. One evening, however, overcome by the passion which, by mutual indulgence, had become resistless, he cast himself at her feet, and, avowing most unbounded love, demanded the promised return. A slight spark of virtue yet burned in the bosom of the wretched girl; she essayed to fly from temptation; but Wolfstein, seizing her hand, said, "And is my adored Megalena a victim then to prejudice? Does she believe, that the Being who created us gave us passions which never were to be satiated? Does she suppose that Nature created us to become the tormentors of each other?"

"Ah! Wolfstein," Megalena said tenderly, "rise!—You know too well the chain which unites me to you is indissoluble; you know that I must be thine; where, therefore, is there an appeal?"

"To thine own heart, Megalena; for, if my image implanted there is not sufficiently eloquent to confirm your hesitating soul, I would wish not for a casket that contains a jewel unworthy of my possession."

Megalena involuntarily started at the strength of his expression; she felt how completely she was his, and turned her eyes upon his countenance, to read in it the meaning of his words.—His eyes gleamed with excessive and confiding love.

"Yes." exclaimed Megalena, "yes, prejudice avaunt! once more reason takes her seat, and convinces me, that to be Wolfstein's is not criminal. O Wolfstein! if for a moment Megalena has yielded to the imbecility of nature, believe that she yet knows how to recover herself, to reappear in her proper character. Ere I knew you, a void in my heart, and a tasteless carelessness of those objects which now interest me, confessed your unseen empire; my heart longed for something which now it has attained. I scruple not, Wolfstein, to aver that it is you:—Be mine, then, and let our affection end not but with our existence!"

"Never, never shall it end!" enthusiastically exclaimed Wolfstein.

"Never!—What can break the bond joined by congeniality of sentiment, cemented by an union of soul which must endure till the intellectual particles which compose it become annihilated? Oh! never shall it end; for when, convulsed by nature's latest ruin, sinks the fabric of this perishable globe; when the earth is dissolved away, and the face of heaven is rolled from before our eyes like a scroll; then will we seek each other, and, in eternal, indivisible, although immaterial union, shall we exist to all eternity."

Yet the love, with which Wolfstein regarded Megalena, notwithstanding the strength of his expressions, though fervent and excessive, at first, was not of that nature which was likely to remain throughout existence; it was like the blaze of the meteor at midnight, which glares amid the darkness for awhile, and then expires; yet did he love her now; at least if heated admiration of her person and accomplishments, independently of mind, be love.

Blessed in mutual affection, if so it may be called, the time passed swift to Wolfstein and Megalena. No incident worthy of narration occurred to disturb the uninterrupted tenour of their existence. Tired, at last, even with delight, which had become monotonous from long continuance, they began to frequent the public places. It was one evening, nearly a month subsequent to their first residence at Genoa, that they went to a party at the Duca di Thice. It was there that he beheld the gaze of one of the crowd fixed upon him. Indefinable to himself were the emotions which shook him; in vain he turned to every part of the saloon to evade the scrutiny of the stranger's gaze; he was not able to give formation, in his own mind, to the ideas which struck him; they were acknowledged, however, in his heart, by sensations awful, and not to be described. He knew that he had before seen the features of the stranger; but he had forgotten Ginotti; for it was Ginotti—from whose scrutinizing glance, Wolfstein turned appalled;—it was Ginotti, of whose strangely and fearfully gleaming eyeball Wolfstein endeavoured to evade the fascination in vain. His eyes, resistlessly attracted to the sphere of chill horror that played around Ginotti's glance, in vain were fixed on vacuity; in vain attempted to notice other objects. Complaining to Megalena of sudden and violent indisposition, Wolfstein with her retired, and they quickly reached the steps of their mansion. Arrived there, Megalena tenderly inquired the cause of Wolfstein's illness, but his vague answers, and unconnected exclamations, soon led her to suppose it was not corporeal. She entreated him to acquaint her with the reason of his indisposition; Wolfstein, however, wishing to conceal from Megalena the true cause of his emotions, evasively told her that he had felt excessively faint from the heat of the assembly; she well knew, by his manner, that he had not told her truth, but affected to be satisfied, resolving, at some future period, to develope the mystery with which he evidently was environed. Retired to rest, Wolfstein's mind, torn by contending paroxysms of passion, admitted not of sleep; he ruminated on the mysterious reappearance of Ginotti; and the more he reflected, the more did the result of his reflections lead him astray. The strange gaze of Ginotti, and the consciousness that he was completely in the power of so indefinable a being; the consciousness that, wheresoever he might go, Ginotti would still follow him, pressed upon Wolfstein's heart. Ignorant of what connexion they could have with this mysterious observer of his actions, his crimes recurred in hideous and disgustful array to the bewildered mind of Wolfstein; he reflected, that, although now exulting in youthful health and vigour, the time would come, the dreadful day of retribution, when endless damnation would yawn beneath his feet, and he would shrink from eternal punishment before the tribunal of that God whom he had insulted. To evade death, unconscious why, became an idea on which he dwelt with earnestness; he thought on it for a time, and being mournfully convinced of its impossibility, strove to change the tenour of his reflections.

While these thoughts dwelt in his mind, sleep crept imperceptibly over his senses; yet, in his visions, was Ginotti present. He dreamed that he stood on the brink of a frightful precipice, at whose base, with deafening and terrific roar, the waves of the ocean dashed; that, above his head, the blue glare of the lightning dispelled the obscurity of midnight, and the loud crashing of the thunder was rolled franticly from rock to rock; that, along the cliff on which he stood, a figure, more frightful than the imagination of man is capable of portraying, advanced towards him, and was about to precipitate him headlong from the summit of the rock whereon he stood, when Ginotti advanced, and rescued him from the grasp of the monster; that no sooner had he done this, than the figure dashed Ginotti from the precipice—his last groans were borne on the blast which swept the bosom of the ocean. Confused visions then obliterated the impressions of the former, and he rose in the morning restless and unrefreshed.

A weight which his utmost efforts could not remove, pressed upon the bosom of Wolfstein; his mind, superior and towering as it was, found all its energies inefficient to conquer it. As a last resource, therefore, this wretched victim of vice and folly sought the gaming-table; a scene which alone could raise the spirits of one who required something important, even in his pastimes, to interest him. He staked large sums; and, although he concealed his haunts from Megalena, she soon discovered them. For a time, fortune smiled; till one evening he entered his mansion, desperate from ill luck, and, accusing his own hapless destiny, could no longer conceal the truth from Megalena. She reproved him mildly, and her tenderness had such an effect on Wolfstein that he burst into tears, and promised her that never again would he yield to the vicious influence of folly.

The rapid days rolled on, and each one brought the conviction to Wolfstein more strongly, that Megalena was not the celestial model of perfection which his warm imagination had portrayed; he began to find in her, not the exhaustless mine of interesting converse which he had once supposed. Possession, which, when unassisted by real, intellectual love, clogs man, increases the ardent, uncontrollable passions of woman even to madness. Megalena yet adored Wolfstein with most fervent love:— although yet greatly attached to Megalena, although he would have been uneasy were she another's, Wolfstein no longer regarded her with that idolatrous affection which had filled his bosom towards her. Feelings of this nature, naturally drove Wolfstein occasionally from home to seek for employment—and what employment, save gaming, could Genoa afford to Wolfstein?—In what other occupation was it possible that he could engage? It was done: he broke his promise to Megalena, and became even a more devoted votary to gambling than before.

How powerful are the attractions of delusive vice! Wolfstein soon staked large sums—larger even than ever. With what anxiety did he watch the dice!—How were his eyeballs strained with mingled anticipation of wealth and poverty! Now fortune smiled; yet he concealed even his good luck from Megalena. At length the tide changed again: he lost immense sums; and, desperate from a series of ill success, cursed his hapless destiny, and with wildest emotions rushed into the street. Again he solemnly swore to Megalena, that never more would he risk their mutual happiness by his folly.

Still, hurried away by the impulse of a burning desire of interesting his deadened feelings, did Wolfstein, false to his promise, seek the gaming-table; he had staked an enormous amount, and the fatal throw was at this instant about to decide the fate of the unhappy Wolfstein.

A pause, as if some dreadful event were about to occur, ensued; each gazed upon the countenance of Wolfstein, which, desperate from danger, retained, however, an expressive firmness.

A stranger stood before Wolfstein on the opposite side of the table. He appeared to have no interest in what was going forward, but, with immoved gaze, fixed his eyes upon his countenance.

Wolfstein felt an instinctive shuddering thrill through his frame, when, oh horrible confirmation of his wildest apprehensions! it was—Ginotti!— the terrible, the mysterious Ginotti, whose dire scrutiny, resting upon Wolfstein, chilled his soul with excessive affright.

A sensation of extreme and conflicting emotions shook the inmost recesses of Wolfstein's heart; for an instant his brain swam around in wildest commotion, yet he steeled his resolution, even to the horrors of hell and destruction; he gazed on the mysterious scrutineer who stood before him, and, regardless of the sum he had staked, and which before had engaged his whole attention, and excited his liveliest interest, dashed the box convulsively upon the table, and followed Ginotti, who was about to quit the apartment, resolving to clear up a fatality which hung around him, and appeared to blast his prospects; for of the misfortunes which had succeeded his association with the bandits, he had not the slightest doubt, in his own mind, that Ginotti was the cause.

With reflections a scene of the wildest anarchy, Wolfstein resolved to unravel the mystery in which he saw Ginotti was shrouded; and resolved, therefore, to devote that night towards finding out his abode. With feelings such as these, he rushed into the street, and followed the gigantic form of Ginotti, who stalked onwards majestically, as if conscious of safety, and wholly ignorant of the eager scrutiny with which Wolfstein watched his every movement.

It was midnight—yet they continued to advance; a feeling of desperation urged Wolfstein onwards; he resolved to follow Ginotti, even to the extremity of the universe. They passed through many bye and narrow streets; the darkness was complete; but the rays of the lamps, as they fell upon the lofty form of Ginotti, guided the footsteps of Wolfstein.

They had reached the end of the Strada Nuova; the lengthened sound of Ginotti's footsteps was all that struck upon Wolfstein's ear. On a sudden, Ginotti's figure disappeared from Wolfstein's gaze; in vain he looked around him, in vain he searched every recess, wherein he might have secreted himself—Ginotti was gone!

To describe the surprise mingled with awe, which possessed Wolfstein's bosom, is impossible. In vain he searched every part. He proceeded to the bridge; a party of fishermen were waiting there; he inquired of them, had they seen a man of superior stature pass? they appeared surprised at his question, and unanimously answered in the negative. While varying emotions tumultuously contended within his bosom, Wolfstein, ever the victim of extraordinary events, paused awhile, revolving the mystery both of Ginotti's appearance and disappearance. That business of an important nature led him to Genoa, he doubted not; his indifference at the gaming-table, his particular regard of Wolfstein, left, in the mind of the latter, no doubt, but that he took a terrible and mysterious interest in whatever related to him.

All now was silent. The inhabitants of Genoa lay wrapped in sleep, and, save the occasional conversation of the fishermen who had just returned, no sound broke on the uninterrupted stillness, and thick clouds obscured the starbeams of heaven.

Again Wolfstein searched that part of the city which lay near Strada Nuova; but no one had seen Ginotti; although all wondered at the wild expressions and disordered mien of Wolfstein. The bell tolled the hour of three ere Wolfstein relinquished his pursuit; finding, however, further inquiry fruitless, he engaged a chair to take him to his habitation, where he doubted not that Megalena anxiously awaited his return.

Proceeding along the streets, the obscurity of the night was not so great but that he observed the figure of one of the chairmen to be above that of common men, and that he had drawn his hat forwards to conceal his countenance. His appearance, however, excited no remark; for Wolfstein was too much absorbed in the idea which related individually to himself, to notice what, perhaps, at another time, might have excited wonder. The wind sighed moaningly along the stilly colonnades, and the grey light of morning began to appear above the eastern eminences.

They entered the street which soon led to the abode of Wolfstein, who fixed his eyes upon the chairman. His gigantic proportions struck him with involuntary awe: such is the unaccountable connexion of idea in the mind of man. He shuddered. Such a man, thought he, is Ginotti:

such a man is he who watches my every action, whose power I feel within myself is resistless, and not to be evaded. He sighed deeply when he reflected on the terrible connexion, dreadful although mysterious, which subsisted between himself and Ginotti. His soul sank within him at the idea of his own littleness, when a fellowmortal might be able to gain so strong, though sightless, an empire over him. He felt that he was no longer independent. Whilst these thoughts agitated his mind, the chair had stopped at his habitation. He turned round to discharge the chairman's fare, when, casting his eyes on his countenance, which hitherto had remained concealed, oh horrible and chilling conviction! he recognised in his dark features those of the terrific Ginotti. As if hell had yawned at the feet of the hapless Wolfstein, as if some spectre of the night had blasted his straining eyeball, so did he stand transfixed. His soul shrank with mingled awe and abhorrence from a being who, even to himself, was confessedly superior to the proud and haughty Wolfstein. Ere well he could calm his faculties, agitated by so unexpected an interview, Ginotti said.

"Wolfstein! long have I known you; long have I marked you as the only man who now exists, worthy, and appreciating the value of what I have in store for you. Inscrutable are my intentions; seek not, therefore, to develope them: time will do it in a far more complete manner. You shall not now know the motive for my, to you, unaccountable actions: strive not, therefore, to unravel them. You may frequently see me: never attempt to speak or follow; for, if you do—" Here the eyes of Ginotti flashed with coruscations of inexpressible fire, and his every feature became animated by the tortures which he was about to describe; but he suddenly checked himself, and only added, "Attend to these my directions, but try, if possible, to forget me. I am not what I seem. The time may come, will most probably arrive, when I shall appear in my real character to you. You, Wolfstein, have I singled out from the whole world to make the depositary—" He ceased, and abruptly quitted the spot.

# IV

*—Nature shrinks back.*
*Enhorror'd from the lurid gaze of vengeance.*
*E'en in the deepest caverns, and the voice*
*Of all her works lies hush'd.*

—Olympia

On Wolfstein's return to his habitation, he found Megalena in anxious expectation of his arrival. She feared that some misfortune had befallen him. Wolfstein related to her the events of the preceding night; they appeared to her mysterious and inexplicable; nor could she offer any consolation to the wretched Wolfstein.

The occurrences of the preceding evening left a load upon his breast, which all the gaieties of Genoa were insufficient to dispel: eagerly he longed for the visit of Ginotti. Slow dragged the hours: each day did he expect it, and each succeeding day brought but disappointment to his expectations.

Megalena too, the beautiful, the adored Megalena, was no longer what formerly she was, the innocent girl hanging on his support, and depending wholly upon him for defence and protection; no longer, with mild and love-beaming eyes, she regarded the haughty Wolfstein as a superior being, whose look or slightest word was sufficient to decide her on any disputed point. No; dissipated pleasures had changed the former mild and innocent Megalena. Far, far different was she than when she threw herself into his arms on their escape from the cavern, and, with a blush, smiled upon the first declaration of Wolfstein's affection.

Now immersed in a succession of gay pleasures, Megalena was no longer the gentle interesting she, whose soul of sensibility would tremble if a worm beneath her feet expired; whose heart would sink within her at the tale of others' woe. She had become a fashionable belle, and forgot, in her new character, the fascinations of her old one. Still, however, was she ardently, solely, and resistlessly attached to Wolfstein: his image was implanted in her soul, never to be effaced by casualty, never erased by time. No coolness apparently took place between them; but, although unperceived and unacknowledged by each, an indifference evidently did exist between them. Among the various families whom their residence in Genoa had rendered familiar to Wolfstein and Megalena, none were more so than that of il Conte della Anzasca; it consisted of himself, la Contessa, and a daughter of exquisite loveliness, named Olympia.

This girl, mistress of every fascinating accomplishment, uniting in herself to great brilliancy and playfulness of wit, a person alluring beyond description, was in her eighteenth year. From habitual indulgence, her passions, naturally violent and excessive, had become irresistible; and when once she had fixed a determination in her mind, that determination must either be effected, or she must cease to exist. Such, then, was the beautiful Olympia, and as such she conceived a violent and unconquerable passion for Wolfstein. His towering and majestic form, his expressive and regular features, beaming with somewhat of softness; yet pregnant with a look as if woe had beat to the earth a mind whose native and unconfined energies aspired to heaven—all, all told her, that, without him, she must either cease to be, or drag on a life of endless and irremediable woe. Nourished by restless imagination, her passion soon attained a most unbridled height: instead of conquering a feeling which honour, generosity, virtue, all forbade ever to be gratified, she gloried within herself at having found one on whom she might with justice fix her burning attachment; for although the object of them had never before been present to her mind, the desires for that object, although unseen, had taken root long, long ago. A false system of education, and a wrong expansion of ideas, as they became formed, had been put in practice with respect to her youthful mind; and indulgence strengthened the passions which it behoved restraint to keep within proper bounds, and which might have unfolded themselves as coadjutors of virtue, and not as promoters of vicious and illicit love. Fiercer, nevertheless, in proportion as greater obstacles appeared in the prosecution of her resolve, flamed the passion of the devoted Olympia. Her brain was whirled round in the fiercest convulsions of expectant happiness; the anticipation of gratified voluptuousness swelled her bosom even to bursting, yet did she rein-in the boiling emotions of her soul, and resolved to be sufficiently cool, more certainly to accomplish her purpose.

It was one night when Wolfstein's mansion was the scene of gaiety, that this idea first suggested itself to the mind of Olympia, and unfolded itself to her, as it really was love for Wolfstein. In vain the suggestions of generosity, the voice of conscience, which told her how doubly wicked would be the attempt of alienating from her the lover of her friend Megalena, in audible, though noiseless, accents spoke; in vain the native modesty of her sex represented in its real and hideous colours what she was about to do: still Olympia was resolved.

That night, in the solitude of her own chamber, in the palazzo of her father, she retraced in her mind the various events which had led to her present uncontrollable passion, which had employed her whole thoughts, and rendered her, as it were, dead to every other outward existence. The wild transports of maddening desire raved terrific within her breast: she endeavoured to smother the ideas which presented themselves; but the more she strove to erase them from her mind, the more vividly were they represented in her heated and enthusiastic imagination. "And will he not return my love?" she exclaimed: "will he not?—ah! a bravo's dagger shall pierce his heart, and thus will I reward him for his contempt of Olympia della Anzasca. But no! it is impossible. I will cast myself at his feet; I will avow to him the passion which consumes me,—will swear to be ever, ever his! Can he then cast me from him? Can he despise a woman whose only fault is love, nay, idolatry, adoration for him?"

She paused.—The tumultuous passions of her soul were now too fierce for utterance—too fierce for concealment or restraint. The hour was late; the moon poured its mildlylustrous beams upon the lengthened colonnades of Genoa, when Olympia, overcome by emotions such as these, quitted her father's palazzo, and hastened, with rapid and unequal footsteps, towards the mansion of Wolfstein. The streets were by no means crowded; but those who yet lingered in them gazed with slight surprise on the figure of Olympia, which, light and symmetrical as a celestial sylphid, passed swiftly onwards.

She soon arrived at the habitation of Wolfstein, and sent the domestic to announce that one wished to speak with him, whose business was pressing and secret. She was conducted into an apartment, and there awaited the arrival of Wolfstein. A confused expression of awe played upon his features as he entered; but it suddenly gave place to that of surprise. He started upon perceiving Olympia, and said.

"To what, Lady Olympia, do I owe the unforeseen pleasure of your visit? What so mysterious business have you with me?" continued he playfully.

"But come, we had just sat down to supper; Megalena is within."— "Oh! if you wish to see me expire in horrible torments at your feet, inhuman Wolfstein, call for Megalena! and then will your purpose be accomplished."—"Dearest Lady Olympia, compose yourself, I beseech you," said Wolfstein: "what, what agitates you?"—"Oh! pardon, pardon me," she exclaimed, with maniac wildness: "pardon a wretched female who knows not what she does! Oh! resistlessly am I impelled to this avowal; resistlessly am I impelled to declare to you, that I love you! adore you to distraction!—Will you return my affection? But, ah! I rave! Megalena, the beloved Megalena, claims you as her own; and the wretched Olympia must moan the blighted prospects which were about to open fair before her eyes."

"For Heaven's sake, dear lady, compose yourself; recollect who you are; recollect the loftiness of birth and loveliness of form which are so eminently yours. This, this is far beneath Olympia."

"Oh!" she exclaimed, franticly casting herself at his feet, and bursting into a passion of tears, "what are birth, fame, fortune, and all the advantages which are casually given to me! I swear to thee, Wolfstein, that I would sacrifice not only these, but even all my hopes of future salvation, even the forgiveness of my Creator, were it required from me. O Wolfstein, kind, pitying Wolfstein, look down with an eye of indulgence on a female whose only crime is resistless, unquenchable adoration of you."

She panted for breath, her pulses beat with violence, her eyes swam, and, overcome by the conflicting passions of her soul, the frame of Olympia fell, sickening with faintness, on the ground. Wolfstein raised her, and tenderly essayed to recall the senses of the hapless girl. Recovering, and perceiving her situation, Olympia started, seemingly horrified, from the arms of Wolfstein. The energies of her high mind instantly resumed their functions, and she exclaimed, "Then, base and ungrateful Wolfstein, you refuse to unite your fate with mine? My love is ardent and excessive, but the revenge which may follow the despiser of it is far more impetuous; reflect well then ere you drive Olympia della Anzasca to despair."—"No reflection, in the present instance, is needed, Lady," replied Wolfstein, coolly, yet determinedly. "What man of honour needs a moment's rumination to discover what nature has so inerasibly implanted in his bosom—the sense of right and wrong? I am connected with a female whom I love, who confides in me; in what manner should I merit her confidence, if I join myself to another? Nor can the loveliness, the exquisite, the unequalled loveliness of the beautiful Olympia della Anzasca compensate me for breaking an oath sworn to another."

He paused.—Olympia spake not, but appeared to be awaiting the dreadful fiat of her destiny.

"Olympia," Wolfstein continued, "pardon me! Were I not irrevocably Megalena's, I must be thine: I esteem you, I admire you, but my love is another's."

The passion which before had choked Olympia's utterance, appeared to give way to the impetuousness of her emotions.

"Then," she said, as a solemnity of despair toned her voice to firmness, "then you are irrevocably another's?"

"I am compelled to be explicit; I am compelled to say, I am another's for ever!" fervently returned Wolfstein.

Again fainting from the excess of painful feeling which vibrated through her frame, Olympia fell at Wolfstein's feet: again he raised her, and, in anxious solicitude, watched her varying countenance. At the critical instant when Olympia had just recovered from the faintness which had oppressed her, the door burst open, and disclosed to the view of the passion-grieving Olympia, the detested form of Megalena. A silence, resembling that when a solemn pause in the midnight-tempest announces that the elements only hesitate to collect more terrific force for the ensuing explosion, took place, while Megalena surveyed Olympia and Wolfstein. Still she spoke not; yet the silence, even more terrible than the commotion which followed, continued to prevail. Olympia dashed by Megalena, and faintly articulating "Vengeance!" rushed into the street, and bent her rapid flight to the Palazzo di Anzasca.

"Wolfstein," said Megalena, her voice quivering with excessive emotion, "Wolfstein, how have I deserved this? How have I deserved a dereliction so barbarous and so unprovoked? But no!" she added in a firmer tone; "no! I will leave you! I will show that I can bear the tortures of disappointed love, better than you can evade the scrunity of one who did adore thee."

In vain Wolfstein put in practice every soothing art of tranquillize the agitation of Megalena. Her frame trembled with violent shuddering; yet her soul, as it were, superior to the form which enshrined it, loftily towered, and retained its firmness amidst the frightful chaos which battled within.

"Now," said she to Wolfstein, "I will leave you!"

"O God! Megalena, dearest, adored Megalena!" exclaimed Wolfstein, passionately, "stop—I love you, must ever love you: deign, at least, to

　　　　　　　　　　　　　　　　PERCY BYSSHE SHELLEY

hear me."—"What good would accrue from that?" gloomily inquired Megalena.

Wolfstein rushed towards her; he threw himself at her feet, and exclaimed, "If ever, for one instant, my soul was alienated from thee—if ever it swerved from the affection which I have sworn to thee—may the red right hand of God instantaneously dash me beneath the lowest abyss of hell! O Megalena! is it as a victim of groundless jealousy that I have immolated myself at the altar of thy perfections? Have I only raised myself to this summit of happiness to feel more deeply the fall of which thou art the cause? O Megalena! if yet one spark of thy former love lingers in thy breast, oh! believe one who swears that he must be thine even till the particles which compose the soul devoted to thee, become annihilated."—He paused.

Megalena heard his wildly enthusiastic expressions in sullen silence. She looked upon him with a stern and severe gaze:—he yet lay at her feet, and, hiding his face upon the earth, groaned deeply. "What proof," exclaimed Magalena, impatiently, "what proof will Wolfstein, the deceiver, bring to satisfy me that his love is still mine?"

"Seek for proof in my heart," returned Wolfstein; "that heart which yet is bleeding from the thorns which thou, cruel girl, hast implanted in it: seek it in my every action, and then will the convinced Megalena know that Wolfstein is hers irrevocably—body and soul, for ever!"

"Yet, I believe thee not!" said Mega lena; "for the haughty Olympia della Anzasca would scarcely recline in the arms of a man who was not entirely devoted to her."

Yet were the charms of Megalena unfaded; yet their empire over Wolfstein excessive and complete.

"Still I believe thee not," continued she, as a smile of expectant malice sat upon her cheek. "I require some proof which will assuredly convince me, that I am yet beloved: give me proof, and Megalena will again be Wolfstein's."—"Oh!" said Wolfstein, mournfully, "what farther proof can I give, but my oath, that never in soul or body have I broken the allegiance that I formerly swore to thee?"

"The death of Olympia!" gloomily returned Megalena.

"What mean you?" said Wolfstein, starting.

"I mean," continued Megalena, collectedly, as if what she was about to utter had been the result of serious cogitation; "I mean that, if ever you wish again to possess my affections, ere to-morrow morning, Olympia must expire!"

"Murder the innocent Olympia?"

"Yes!"

A pause ensued; during which the mind of Wolfstein, torn by ten thousand warring emotions, knew not on what to resolve. He gazed upon Megalena; her symmetrical form shone with tenfold loveliness to his enraptured imagination: again he resolved to behold those eyes beam with affection for him, which were now gloomily fixed upon the ground. "Will nothing else convince Megalena that Wolfstein is eternally hers?"

"Nothing."

"'T is done then," exclaimed Wolfstein, "'t is done. Yet," he muttered, "I may suffer for this premeditated act tortures now inconceivable; I may writhe, convulsed, in immaterial agony for ever and for ever— ah! I cannot. No!" he continued; "Megalena, I am again yours; I will immolate the victim which thou requirest as a sacrifice to our love. Give me a dagger, which may sweep off from the face of the earth, one who is hateful to thee! Adored creature, give me the dagger, and I will restore it to thee dripping with Olympia's hated blood; it shall have first been buried in her heart."

"Then, then again art thou mine own! again art thou the idolized Wolfstein, whom I was wont to love!" said Megalena, enfolding him in her embrace. Perceiving her returning softness, Wolfstein essayed to induce her to spare him the frightful proof of the ardour of his attachment; but she started from his arms as he spoke, and exclaimed.

"Ah! base deceiver, do you hesitate?"

"Oh, no! I do not hesitate, dearest Megalena;—give me a dagger, and I go."

"Here, follow me then," returned Megalena. He followed her to the supper-room.

"It is useless to go yet, it has but yet struck one; the inhabitants of il Palazzo della Anzasca will, about two, be nearly all retired to rest; till then, let us converse on what we were about to do." So far did Megalena's seductive blandishment, her artful selection of converse, win upon Wolfstein, that, when the destined hour approached, his sanguinary soul thirsted for the blood of the comparatively innocent Olympia.

"Well!" he cried, swallowing down an overflowing goblet of wine, "now the time is come; now suffer me to go, and tear the soul of Olympia from her hated body." His fury amounted almost to delirium, as, masked, and having a dagger, which Megalena had given him, concealed beneath his garments, he proceeded rapidly along the streets towards the Palazzo della Anzasca. So eager was he to shed the lifeblood of Olympia, that he flew, rather than ran, along the silent streets of Genoa. The colonnades of the lofty Palazzo della Anzasca resounded to his rapid footsteps; he stopped at its lofty portal:—it was open; unperceived he entered, and, hiding himself behind a column, according to the directions of Megalena, waited there. Soon advancing through the hall, he saw the sylphlike figure of the lovely Olympia; with silent tread he followed it, experiencing not the slightest sentiment of remorse within his bosom for the deed which he was about to perpetrate. He followed her to her apartment, and secreting himself until Olympia might have sunk into sleep, with sanguinary and remorseless patience, when her loud breathing convinced him that her slumber was profound, he arose from his place of concealment, and advanced to the bed, wherein Olympia lay. Her light tresses, disengaged from the band which had confined them, floated around a countenance, superhumanly beautiful, and whose expression, even in slumber, appeared to be tinted by Wolfstein's refusal; convulsive sighs heaved her fair bosom, and tears, starting from under her eyelids, fell profusely down her damask cheek. Wolfstein gazed upon her in silence. "Cruel, inhuman Megalena!" he mentally soliloquized; "could nothing but immolation of this innocence appease thee?" Again he stifled the stings of rebelling conscience; again the unquenchable and resistless ardour of his love for Megalena stimulated him to the wildest pitch of fury: he raised high the dagger, and, drawing aside the covering which veiled her alabaster bosom, paused an instant, to decide in which place it were most instantaneously destructive to strike. Again a mournful smile irradiated her lovely features; it played with a sweet softness on her countenance: it seemed as though she smiled in defiance of the arrows of destiny, but that her soul, nevertheless, lingered with the wretch who sought her life. Maddened by the sight of so much beauteous innocence, even the desperate Wolfstein, forgetful of the danger which he must thereby incur, hurled the dagger from him. The sound awakened Olympia: she started up in surprise; but her alarm was changed into ecstacy when she beheld the idolized possessor of her soul standing before her.

"I was dreaming of you," said Olympia, scarcely knowing whether this were not a dream; but, impulsively following the first emotions of her soul, "I dreamed that you were about to murder me. It is not so, Wolfstein, no! you would not murder one who adores you?"

"Murder Olympia! O God! no!—I take Heaven to witness, that I never now could do it!"

"Nor could you ever, I hope, dear Wolfstein; but drive away thoughts like these, and remember that Olympia lives but for thee; and the moment which takes from her your affections, seals the death-like fiat of her destiny." These asseverations, strengthened by the most solemn and deadly vows that he would return to Megalena the destroyer of Olympia, flashed across Wolfstein's mind. Perpetrate the deed, now, he could not; his soul became a scene of most terrific agony. "Wilt thou be mine?" exclaimed the enraptured Olympia, as a ray of hope arose in her mind. "Never! never can I," groaned the agitated Wolfstein; "I am irrevocably, indissolubly another's." Maddened by this death-blow to all expectations of happiness, which the deluded Olympia had so fondly anticipated, she leaped wildly from the bed. A light and flowing night-dress alone veiled her form: her alabaster bosom was shaded by the light ringlets of her hair which rested unconfined upon it. She threw herself at the feet of Wolfstein. On a sudden, as if struck by some thought, she started convulsively from the earth: for an instant she paused.

The rays of a lamp, which stood in a recess of the apartment, fell full upon the dagger of Wolfstein. Eagerly Olympia sprung towards it; and, ere Wolfstein was aware of her dreadful intent, plunged it into her bosom. Weltering in purple gore she fell: no groan, no sigh escaped her lips. A smile, which the pangs of dissolution could not dispel, played on her convulsed countenance; it irradiated her features with celestially awful, although terrific expression. "Ineffectually have I endeavoured to conquer the ardent feelings of my soul; now I overcome them," were her last words. She utterred them in a tone of firmness, and, falling back, expired in torments, which her fine, her expressive features declared that she gloried in.

All was silent in the chamber of death: the stillness was frightful. The agonies which Wolfstein endured were past description: for a time he neither moved nor spoke. The pale glare of the lamp fell upon the features of Olympia, from which the tinge of life had fled for ever. Suddenly, and in despite of himself, were the affections of Wolfstein turned from Megalena: he could not but now regard her as a fiend, who had been the cause of Olympia's destruction; who had urged him to a deed from which his nature now shrunk as from annihilation. A wild paroxysm of awful alarm seized upon him: he knelt by the side of

Olympia's corpse; he kissed it, bathed it with his tears, and imprecated a thousand curses on himself. Her features, although convulsed by the agonies of violent dissolution, retained an unchanging image of loveliness, which never might fade away. Her beautiful bosom, in which her hand yet held the fatal dagger, was discoloured with blood, and those affection-beaming orbs were now closed in the never-ending slumber of the grave. Unable longer to endure a sight of so much horror, Wolfstein started up, and, forgetful of every thing save the frightful deed which he had witnessed, rushed from the Palazzo della Anzasca, and mechanically retraced his way towards his own habitation.

Not once that night had Megalena closed her eyes. Her infuriate passions had wound her soul up to a deadly calmness of expectation. She had not, during the whole of the night, retired to rest, but sat, with sanguinary patience, cursing the lagging hours that they passed so slowly, and waiting to hear tidings of death. Morning had begun to streak the eastern sky with gray, when Wolfstein hurried into the supper-room, where Megalena still sat, wildly exclaiming "The deed is done!" Megalena entreated him to be calm, and, more collectedly, to communicate the events which had occurred during the night.

"In the first place," he said in an accent of feigned horror, "the officers of justice are alarmed!"

Deadly affright chilled the soul of Megalena: she turned pale, and, gasping for breath, inquired eagerly respecting the success of his attempt.

"O God!" exclaimed Wolfstein, "that has succeeded but too well! the hapless Olympia welters in her life-blood!"

"Joy! joy!" frantically exclaimed Megalena, her eagerness for revenge overcoming, for the moment, every other feeling.

"But, Megalena," continued Wolfstein, "she fell not by my hand: no, she smiled on me in her sleep, and, when she awoke, finding me deaf to her solicitations, snatched my dagger, and buried it in her bosom."

"Did you wish to prevent the deed?" inquired Megalena.

"Oh! good God of Heaven! thou knowest my heart: I would sacrifice every remaining earthly good were Olympia again alive!"

Megalena spoke not, but a smile of exquisitely gratified malice illumined her features with terrific flame.

"We must instantly quit Genoa," said Wolfstein: "the name on the mask which I left in the Palazzo della Anzasca, will remove all doubt that I was the murderer of Olympia. Yet indeed I care not much for death; if you will it so, Megalena, we will even, as it is, remain in Genoa."

"Oh! no, no!" eagerly cried Megalena: "Wolfstein, I love you beyond expression, and Genoa is destruction; let us seek, therefore, some retired spot, where we may for a while at least secrete ourselves. But, Wolfstein, are you persuaded that I love you? need there more proof be required than that I wished the death of another for thee? it was on that account alone that I desired the destruction of Olympia, that thou mightest be more completely and irresistibly mine."

Wolfstein answered not: the feelings of his soul were far different; the expression of his countenance plainly evinced them: and Megalena regretted that her effervescent passions should have led her to so rash an avowal of her contempt of virtue. They then separated to arrange their affairs, prior to their departure, which, on account of the pressing necessity of the case, must take place immediately. They took with them but two domestics, and, collecting all their stock of money, they were soon far from pursuit and Genoa.

*Yes! 't is the influence of that sightless fiend*
*Who guides my every footstep, that I feel:*
*An iron grasp arrests each fluttering sense.*
*And a fell voice howls in mine anguish'd ear.*
*"Wretch, thou mayst rest no more."*

—Olympia

How sweet are the scenes endeared to us by ideas which we have cherished in the society of one we have loved! How melancholy to wander amongst them again after an absence, perhaps of years; years which have changed the tenour of our existence,—have changed even the friend, the dear friend, for whose sake alone the landscape lives in the memory, for whose sake tears flow at the each varying feature of the scenery, which catches the eye of one who has never seen them since he saw them with the being who was dear to him!

Dark, autumnal, and gloomy was the hour; the winds whistled hollow, and over the expanse of heaven was spread an unvarying sombreness of vapour: nothing was heard save the melancholy shriekings of the night-bird, which, soaring on the evening blast, broke the stillness of the scene, interrupting the meditations of frenzied enthusiasm; mingled with the sighing of the wind, which swept in languid and varying cadence amidst the leafless boughs.

Ah! of whom shall the poor outcast wanderer demand protection? Far, far has she wandered. The vice and unkindness of the world hath torn her tender heart. In whose bosom shall she repose the secret of her sufferings? Who will listen with pity to the narrative of her woe, and heal the wounds which the selfish unkindness of man hath made, and then sent her with them, unbound, on the wide and pitiless world? Lives there one whose confidence the sufferer might seek?

Cold and dreary was the night: November's blast had chilled the air. Is the blast so pitiless as ingratitude and selfishness? Ah, no! thought the wanderer; it is unkind indeed, but not so unkind as that. Poor Eloise de St. Irvyne! many, many are in thy situation; but few have a heart so full of sensibility and excellence for the demoniac malice of man to deform, and then glut itself with hellish pleasure in the conviction of having ravaged the most lovely of the works of their Creator. She gazed upon the sky: the moon had just risen; its full orb was occasionally shaded by a passing cloud: it rose from behind the turrets of le Chateau de St. Irvyne. The poor girl raised her eyes towards it, streaming with tears: she scarce could recognise the once-loved building. She thanked God for permitting her again to behold it; and hastened on with steps tottering from fatigue, yet nerved with the sanguineness of anticipation.

Yes, St. Irvyne was the same as when she had left it five years ago. The same ivy mantled the western tower; the same jasmine which bloomed so luxuriantly when she left it, was still there, though leafless from the season. Thus was it with poor Eloise: she had left St. Irvyne, blooming, and caressed by every one; she returned to it pale, downcast, and friendless. The jasmine encircled the twisted pillars which supported the portal. Alas! whose assistance had prevented Eloise from sinking to the earth?—no one's. She knocked at the door—it was opened, and an instant's space beheld her in the arms of a beloved sister. Needless were it to describe the mutual pleasure, needless to describe the delight, of recognition; suffice it to say, that Eloise once more enjoyed the society of her dearest friend; and, in the happiness of her society, forgot the horrors which had preceded her return to St. Irvyne.

Now were it well for a while to leave Eloise at St. Irvyne, and retrace the events which, since five years, had so darkly tinged the fate of the unsuspecting female, who trusted to the promises of man. It was a beautiful morning in May, and the loveliness of the season had spread a deeper shade of gloom over the features of Eloise, for she knew that not long would her mother live. They journeyed on towards Geneva, whither the physicians had ordered Madame de St. Irvyne to repair, as the last resort of a hope that she might, thereby, escape a rapid decline. On account of the illness of her mother, they proceeded slowly; and ere long they had entered the region of the Alps, the shades of evening, which rapidly began to increase, announced approaching night. They had expected, before this time, to have reached a town; but, either owing to a miscalculation of their route, or the remissness of the postillion, they had not yet done so. The majestic moon which hung above their heads, tinged with silver the fleecy clouds which skirted the far-seen horizon; and, borne on the soft wing of the evening zephyr, shadowy lines of vapour, at intervals, crossed her orbit; then vanishing into the dark blue expansiveness of ether, their fantastic forms, like the phantoms of midnight, became invisible. Now might we almost suppose, that the sightless spirits of the departed good, enthroned on the genial breeze of night, watched over those whom they had loved on earth, and poured into the bosom, to the dictates of which, in this world, they had listened with idolatrous attention, that tranquillity and confidence in the goodness of the Creator, which is necessary for us to experience ere we go to the next. Such tranquillity felt Madame de St. Irvyne: she tried to stifle the ideas which arose within her mind; but the more she strove to repress them, in the more vivid characters were they imprinted on the imagination.

Now had they gained the summit of the mountain, when, suddenly, a crash announced that the carriage had given way.

"What is to be done?" inquired Eloise. The postillion appeared to take no notice of her question. "What is to be done?" again she inquired.

"Why, I scarcely know," answered the postillion; "but 't is impossible to proceed."

"Is there no house nearer than—"

"Oh yes," replied he; "here is a house quite near, but a little out of the way; and, perhaps, Ma'am'selle will not—"

"Oh, lead on, lead on to it," quickly rejoined Eloise.

They followed the postillion, and soon arrived at the house. It was large and plain; and although there were lights in some of the windows, it bore an indefinable appearance of desolation.

In a large hall sat three or four men, whose marked countenances almost announced their profession to be bandits. One of superior and commanding figure whispering to the rest, and himself advancing with the utmost and most unexpected politeness, accosted the travellers. For the ideas with which the countenance of this man inspired Eloise she in vain endeavoured to account. It appeared to her that she had seen him before; that the deep tone of his voice was known to her; and that eye, scintillating with a coruscation of mingled sternness and surprise, found some counterpart in herself. Of gigantic stature, yet formed in the mould of exactest symmetry, was the figure of the stranger who sate before Eloise. His countenance of excessive beauty even, but dark, emanated with an expression of superhuman loveliness; not that grace which may freely be admired, but acknowledged in the inmost soul by sensations mysterious, and before unexperienced. He tenderly inquired, whether the night air had injured the ladies, and pressed them to partake of a repast which the other three men had prepared; he appeared to unbend a severity, which evidently was habitual, and by extreme brilliancy and playfulness of wit, joined to talents for conversation, possessed by few, made Madame de St. Irvyne forget that she was dying; and her daughter, as in rapturous attention she listened to each accent of the stranger, remembered no more that she was about to lose her mother.

In the stranger's society, they almost forgot the lapse of time: a pause in the conversation at last occurred.

"Can Ma'am'selle sing?" inquired the stranger.

"I can," replied Eloise; "and with pleasure."

### Song

*How swiftly through heaven's wide expanse*
*Bright day's resplendent colours fade!*
*How sweetly does the moonbeam's glance*
*With silver tint St. Irvyne's glade!*
*No cloud along the spangled air.*
*Is borne upon the evening breeze;*
*How solemn is the scene! how fair*
*The moonbeams rest upon the trees!*
*Yon dark gray turret glimmers white.*
*Upon it sits the mournful owl;*
*Along the stillness of the night.*
*Her melancholy shriekings roll.*
*But not alone on Irvyne's tower.*
*The silver moonbeam pours her ray;*
*It gleams upon the ivied bower.*
*It dances in the cascade's spray.*
*"Ah! why do dark'ning shades conceal*
*The hour, when man must cease to be?*
*Why may not human minds unveil*
*The dim mists of futurity?*
*"The keenness of the world hath torn*
*The heart which opens to its blast;*
*Despis'd, neglected, and forlorn.*
*Sinks the wretch in death at last."*

She ceased;—the thrilling accents of her interestingly sweet voice died away in the vacancy of stillness;—yet listened the charmed auditors; their imaginations prolonged the tender strain; the uncouth attendants of the stranger were chained in silence, and the enthusiastic gaze of their host was fixed upon the timid countenance of Eloise with wild and mysterious expression. It seemed to say to Eloise, "We meet again;"—and, as the idea struck her imagination, convulsed by a feeling of indescribable and excessive awe, she started.

At last, the hour being late, they all retired. Eloise sought the couch prepared for her; her mind, perturbed by emotions, the cause of which she in vain essayed to develope, could bring its intellectual energies to act on no one particular point; her imagination was fertile, and, under its fantastic guidance, she felt her judgment and reason irresistibly fettered. The image of the fascinating, yet awful stranger, dwelt on her mind. She sank on her knees to return thanks to her Creator for his mercies; yet even then, faithless to the task on which it was employed, her mind returned to the stranger. She felt no particular affection or esteem for him;—no, she rather feared him; and, when she endeavoured to connect the chain of ideas which pressed upon her mind, tears started into her eyes, and she looked around the apartment with the timid terror of a person who converses at midnight on a subject at once awful and interesting: but poor Eloise was no philosopher; and to explain sensations like these, were even beyond the power of the wisest of them. She felt alarmed, herself, at the violence of the feelings which shook her bosom, and attempted to compose herself to sleep. Yet even in her dream was the stranger present. She thought that she met him on a flowery plain; that the feelings of her bosom, whether she would or not, impelled her towards him; that before she had been enfolded in his arms, a torrent of scintillating flame, accompanied by a terrific crash of thunder, made the earth yawn beneath her feet;—the gay vision vanished from her fancy, and, in place of the flowery plain, a rugged and desolate heath extended far before her; its monotonous solitude unbroken, save by the low and barren rocks which rose occasionally from its surface. From dreams such as these, dreams which left on her mind painful presentiments of her future life, Eloise arose, restless and unrefreshed from slumber.

Why gleams that dark eyeball upon the countenance of Eloise, as she tenderly inquired for the health of her mother? Why did an hidden expression of exulting joy light up that demoniac gaze, when Madame de St. Irvyne said to her daughter, "I feel rather faint to-day, my child:— 'Would we were at Geneva!"—It beams with hell and destruction!—Let me look again: that, when I see another eye which gleams so fiendishly, I may know that it is a villain's.—Thus might have thought the sightless minister of the beneficence of God, as it hovered round the spotless Eloise. But, hush! what was that scream which was heard by the ear of listening enthusiasm? It was the shriek of the fair Eloise's better genius; it screamed to see the foe of the innocent girl so near—it is fled fast to Geneva. "There, Eloise, will we meet again," methought it whispered; whilst a low hollow tone, hoarse from the dank vapours of the grave, seemed lowly to howl in the ear of rapt Fancy, "We meet again likewise."

Their courteous host conducted Madame de St. Irvyne and Eloise to their chaise, which was now repaired, and ready for the journey; the stranger bowed respectfully as they went away. The expression of his dark eye, as he beheld them for the last time, was even stronger than ever; it seemed not to affect her mother; but the mystic feelings which it excited in the bosom of Eloise were beyond description powerful. The paleness of Madame de St. Irvyne's cheek, on which the only teint was an occasional and hectic flush, announced that the illness which consumed her, rapidly increased, and would soon lead her gently to the gates of death. She talked calmly of her approaching dissolution, and only regretted, that to no one protector could she entrust the care of her orphaned daughters. Marianne, her eldest daughter, had, by her mother's particular desire, remained at the chateau; and, though much wishing to accompany her mother, she urged it no longer, when she knew Madame de St. Irvyne to be resolved against it. Now had the illness which had attacked her assumed so serious and so decided an appearance, that she could no longer doubt the event;—could no longer doubt that she was quickly about to enter a better world.

"My daughter," said she, "there is a banker at Geneva, a worthy man, to whom I shall bequeath the guardianship of my child; on that head are all my doubts quieted. But, Eloise, my child, you are yet young; you know not the world; but bear in mind these words of your dying mother, so long as you remember herself:—When you see a man enveloped in deceit and mystery; when you see him dark, reserved, and suspicious, carefully avoid him. Should such a man seek your friendship or affection, should he seek, by any means, to confer an obligation upon you, or make you confer one on him, spurn him from you as you would a serpent; as one who aimed to lure your unsuspecting innocence to the paths of destruction."

The affecting solemnity of her voice, as thus she spoke, touched

Eloise deeply; she wept. "I must remember my mother for ever," was her almost inarticulate reply; deep sobs burst from her agitated bosom; and the varying crowds of imagery which followed each other in her mind, were too complicated to be defined. Still, though deeply grieved at the approaching death of her mother, was the mysterious stranger uppermost in her thoughts; his image excited ideas painful and unpleasant. She wished to turn the tide of them; but the more she attempted it, with the more painful recurrence of almost mechanical force, did his recollection press upon her disturbed intellect.

Eloise de St. Irvyne was a girl, whose temper and disposition was most excellent; she was, indeed, too, possessed of uncommon sensibility; yet was her mind moulded in an inferior degree of perfection. She was susceptible of prejudice, to a great degree; and resigned herself, careless of the consequences which might follow, to the feelings of the moment. Every accomplishment, it is true, she enjoyed in the highest excellence; and the very convent at which she was educated, which afforded the adventitious advantages so highly esteemed by the world, prevented her mind from obtaining that degree of expansiveness and excellence, which, otherwise, might have rendered Eloise nearer approaching to perfection; the very routine of a convent education gave a false and pernicious bias to the ideas, as, luxuriant in youth, they unfolded themselves; and those sentiments which, had they been allowed to take the turn which nature intended, would have become coadjutors of virtue, and strengtheners of that mind, which now they had rendered comparatively imbecile. Such was Eloise, and as such she required unexampled care to prevent those feelings which agitate every mind of sensibility, to get the better of the judgment which had, by an erroneous system of education, become relaxed. Her mother was about to die—who now would care for Eloise?

They entered Geneva at the close of a fine, yet sultry day. The illness of Madame de St. Irvyne had increased so as now to threaten instant danger: she was conveyed to bed. A deadly paleness sat on her cheek; it was flushed, however, as she spoke, with momentary hectics; and, as she conversed with her daughter, a fire, which almost partook of etheriality, shone in her sunken eye. It was evening; the yellow beams of the sun, as his orb shed the parting glory on the verge of the horizon, penetrated the bed-curtains; and by their effulgence contrasted the deadliness of her countenance. The poor Eloise sat, watching, with eyes dimmed by tears, each variation in the countenance of her mother. Silent, from an ecstacy of grief, she gazed fixedly upon her, and felt every earthly hope die within her, when the conviction of a fast-approaching dissolution pressed upon her disturbed brain. Madame de St. Irvyne, at length exhausted, fell into a quiet slumber; Eloise feared to disturb her, but, motionless with grief, sate behind the curtain. Now had sunk the orb of day, and the shades of twilight began to scatter duskiness through the chamber of death; all was silent; and, save by the catchings of breath in her mother's slumber, the stillness was uninterrupted. Yet even in this awful, this terrific crisis of her existence, the mind of Eloise seemed compelled to exert its intellectual energies but on one subject;—in vain she essayed to pray;—in vain she attempted to avert the horror of her meditations, by contemplating the pallid features of her dying mother: her thoughts were not within her own control, and she trembled as she reflected on the appalling and mysterious influence which the image of a man, whom she had seen but once, and whom she neither loved nor cared for, had gained over her mind. With the indefinable terror of one who dreads to behold some phantom, Eloise fearfully cast her eyes around the gloomy apartment; occasionally she shrank from the ideal form which an unconnected imagination had conjured up, and could scarcely but suppose that the stranger's gaze, as last he had looked upon her, met her own with an horrible and mixed scintillation of mysterious cunning and interest. She felt no prepossession in his favour; she rather detested him, and gladly would never have again beheld him; yet, were the circumstances which introduced him to their notice alluded to, she would turn pale, and blush, by turns; and Jeanette, their maid, was fully persuaded in her own mind, and prided herself on her penetration in the discovery, that Ma'am'selle was violently in love with the hospitable Alpine hunter.

Madame de St. Irvyne had now awakened; she beckoned her daughter to approach: Eloise obeyed; and, kneeling, kissed the chill hand of her mother, in a transport of sorrow, and bathed it with her tears.

"Eloise," said her mother, her voice trembling from excessive weakness, "Eloise, my child, farewell—farewell for ever. I feel, I am about to die; but, before I die, willingly would I say much to my dearest daughter. You are now left on the hardhearted, pitiless world; and perhaps, oh! perhaps, about to become an immolated victim of its treachery. Oh!—" Here, overcome by extreme pain, she fell backwards; a transient gleam of animation lighted up her expressive countenance; she smiled, and—expired. All was still; and over the gloomy chamber reigned silence and horror. The yellow moonbeam, with sepulchral effulgence, gleamed on the countenance of her who had expired, and lighted her features, sweet even in death, with a dire and horrible contrast to the dimness which prevailed around!—Ah! such was the contrast of the peace enjoyed by the spirit of the departed one, with the misery which awaited the wretched Eloise. Poor Eloise! she had now lost almost her only friend!

In excessive and silent grief, knelt the mourning girl; she spoke not, she wept-not; her sorrow was toavo violent for tears, but, oh! her heart was torn by pangs of unspeakable acuteness. But even amid the alarm which so melancholy an event must have excited, the idea of the stranger in the Alps sublimed the soul of Eloise to the highest degree of horror, and despair the most infuriate. For the ideas which crowded into her mind at this crisis, so eventful, so terrific, she endeavoured to account; but, alas! her attempt was fruitless! Still knelt she; still did she press to her burning lips the lifeless hand of departed excellence, when the morning's ray announced to her, that longer continuing there might excite suspicion of intellectual derangement. She arose, therefore, and, quitting the apartment, announced the melancholy event which had taken place. She gave orders for the funeral; it was to be solemnized as soon as decency would permit, as the poor friendless Eloise wished speedily to quit Geneva. She wrote to announce the fatal event to her sister. Slowly dragged the time. Eloise followed to its latest bed, the corpse of her mother, and was returning from the convent, when a stranger put into her hand a note, and quickly disappeared:—

"Will Eloise de St. Irvyne meet her friend at—Abbey, to-morrow night, at ten o'clock?"

# VI

*—Why then unbidden gush'd the tear?—*
*Then would cold shudderings seize his brain.*
*As gasping he labour'd for breath;*
*The strange gaze of his meteor eye.*
*Which, frenzied, and rolling dreadfully.*
*Glar'd with hideous gleam.*
*Would chill like the spectre gaze of Death.*
*As, conjur'd by feverish dream.*
*He seems o'er the sick man's couch to stand.*
*And shakes the fell lance in his skeleton hand.*

—Wandering Jew

Yes;—they fled from Genoa; they had eluded pursuit and justice, but could not escape the torments of an outraged and avenging conscience, which, with stings the most acute, pursued them whithersoever they might go. Fortune even seemed to favour them; for fortune will, sometimes, in this world, appear to side with the wicked. Wolfstein had received notice, that an uncle, possessed of immense wealth, had died in Bohemia, and bequeathed to him the whole of his estate. Thither then, with Megalena, went Wolfstein. Their journey produced no event of consequence; suffice it to say, that they arrived at the spot where Wolfstein's new possessions were situated.

Dark and desolate were the scenes which surrounded the no less desolate castle. Gloomy heaths, in unvarying sadness of immensity, stretched far and wide. A scathed pine or oak, blasted by the thunderbolts of heaven, alone broke the monotonous sameness of the imagery. Needless were it to describe the castle, built like all those of the Bohemian barons, in mingled Gothic and barbarian architecture. Over the dark expanse the dim moon beaming, and faintly, with its sepulchral radiance, dispersing the thickness of the vapours which lowered around (for her waning horn, which hung low above the horizon, added but tenfold horror to the terrific desolation of the scene); the night-raven pouring on the dull ear of evening her frightful screams, and breaking on the otherwise uninterrupted stillness,—were the melancholy greetings to their new habitation.

PERCY BYSSHE SHELLEY

They alighted at the antique entrance, and, passing through a vast and comfortless hall, were conducted into a saloon not much less so. The coolness of the evening, for it was late in the autumn, made the wood fire, which had been lighted, disperse a degree of comfort; and Wolfstein, having arranged his domestic concerns, continued talking with Megalena until midnight.

"But you have never yet correctly explained to me," said Megalena, "the mystery which encircled that strange man whom we met at the inn at Breno. I think I have seen him once since, or I should not now have thought of the circumstance."

"Indeed, Megalena, I know of no mystery. I suppose the man was mad, or wished to make us think so; for my part, I have never thought of him since; nor ever intend to think of him."

"Do you not?" exclaimed a voice, which enchained motionless to his seat the horror-struck Wolfstein—when turning round, and starting in agonized frenzy from his chair, Ginotti himself—Ginotti—from whose terrific gaze never had he turned unappalled, stood in cool and fearless contempt before him!

"Do you not?" continued the mysterious stranger." Never again intendest thou to think of me?—me! who have watched each expanding idea, conscious to what I was about to apply them, conscious of the great purpose for which each was formed. Ah! Wolfstein, by my agency shalt thou—" He paused, assuming a smile expressive of exultation and superiority.

"Oh! do with me what thou wilt, strange, inexplicable being!— Do with me what thou wilt!" exclaimed Wolfstein, as an ecstacy of frenzied terror overpowered his astonished senses. Megalena still sat unmoved: she was surprised, it is true; but most was she surprised, that an event like this should have power so to shake Wolfstein; for even then he stood gazing in enhorrored silence on the majestic figure of Ginotti.

"Fool, then, that thou art, to deny me!" continued Ginotti, in a tone less solemn, but more severe. "Wilt thou promise me that, when I come to demand what thou covenantedst with me at Breno, I meet no fears, no scruples, but that, then, thou wilt perform what there thou didst swear, and that this oath shall be inviolable?"

"It shall," replied Wolfstein.

"Swear it."

"As I keep my vows with you, may God reward me hereafter!"

"'Tis done then," returned Ginotti. "Ere long shall I claim the performance of this covenant—now farewell." Speaking thus, Ginotti dashed away; and, mounting a horse which stood at the gate, sped swiftly across the heath. His form lessened in the clear moonlight; and, when it was no longer visible to the straining eyeballs of Wolfstein, he felt, as it were, a spell which had enthralled him, to be dissolved.

Reckless of Megalena's earnest entreaties, he threw himself into a chair, in deep and gloomy melancholy; he answered them not, but, immersed in a train of corroding ideas, remained silent. Even when retired to repose, and he could, occasionally, sink into a transitory slumber, would he again start from it, as he thought that Ginotti's majestic form leaned over him, and that the glance which, last, his fearful eye had thrown, chilled his breast with indescribable agony. Slowly lagged the time to Wolfstein; Ginotti, though now gone, and far away perhaps, dwelt in his disturbed mind; his image was there imprinted in characters terrific and indelible. Oft would he wander along the desolate heath; on every blast of wind which sighed over the scattered remnants of what was once a forest, Ginotti's, the terrific Ginotti's voice seemed to float; and in every dusky recess, favoured by the descending shades of gloomy night, his form appeared to lurk, and, with frightful glare, his eye to penetrate the conscience-stricken Wolfstein as he walked. A falling leaf, or a hare starting from her heathy seat, caused him to shrink with affright; yet, though dreading loneliness, he was irresistibly compelled to seek for solitude. Megalena's charms had now no longer power to speak comfort to his soul: ephemeral are the friendships of the wicked, and involuntary disgust follows the attachment founded on the visionary fabric of passion or interest. It sinks in the merited abyss of ennui, or is followed by apathy and carelessness, which amply its origin deserved.

The once ardent and excessive passion of Wolfstein for Megalena, was now changed into disgust and almost detestation; he sought to conceal it from her, but it was evident, in spite of his resolution. He regarded her as a woman capable of the most shocking enormities; since, without any adequate temptation to vice, she had become sufficiently depraved to consider an inconsequent crime the wilful and premeditated destruction of a fellow-creature; still, whether it were from the indolence which he had contracted, or an indefinably sympathetic connexion of soul, which forbade them to part during their mortal existence, was Wolfstein irremediably linked to his mistress, who was as depraved as himself, though originally of a better disposition. He likewise had, at first, resisted the allurements of vice; but, overpowered by its incitements, had resigned himself, indeed reluctantly, to its influence. But Megalena had courted its advances, and endeavoured to conquer neither the suggestions of crime, nor the dictates of a nature prone to the attacks of appetite—let me not call it passion.

Fast advanced winter: cheerless and solitary were the days. Wolfstein, occasionally, followed the chase; but even that was wearisome: and the bleeding image of the murdered Olympia, or the still more dreaded idea of the terrific Ginotti, haunted him in the midst of its tumultuous pleasures, and embittered every instant of his existence. The pale corpse too of Cavigni, blackened by poison, reigned in his chaotic imagination, and stung his soul with tenfold remorse, when he reflected that he had murdered one who never had injured him, for the sake of a being whose depraved society every succeeding day rendered more monotonous and insipid.

It was one evening when, according to his custom, Wolfstein wandered late: it was in the beginning of December, and the weather was peculiarly mild for the season and latitude. Over the cerulean expanse of ether the dim moon, shrouded in the fleeting fragments of vapour, which, borne on the pinions of the northern blast, crossed her pale orb; at intervals, the dismal hooting of the owl, which, searching for prey, flitted her white wings over the dusky heath; the silver beams which slept on the outline of the far-seen forests, and the melancholy stillness, uninterrupted save by these concomitants of gloom, conduced to sombre reflection. Wolfstein reclined upon the heath; he retraced, in mental review, the past events of his life, and shuddered at the darkness of his future destiny. He strove to repent of his crimes; but, though conscious of the connexion which existed between the ideas, as often as repentance presented itself to his mind, Ginotti rushed upon his troubled imagination, and a dark veil seemed to separate him for ever from contrition, notwithstanding he was constantly subjected to the tortures inflicted by it. At last, wearied with the corroding recollections, the acme of which progressively increased, he bent his steps again towards his habitation.

As he was entering the portal, a grasp of iron arrested his arm, and, turning round, he recognised the tall figure of Ginotti, which enveloped in a mantle, had leaned against a jutting buttress. Amazement, for a time, chained the faculties of Wolfstein in motionless surprise: at last he recollected himself, and, in a voice trembling from agitation, inquired, did he now demand the performance of the promise?

"I come," he said, "I come to demand it, Wolfstein! Art thou willing to perform what thou hast promised?—but come—"

A degree of solemnity, mixed with concealed fierceness, toned his voice as he spoke; yet was he fixed in the attitude in which first he had addressed Wolfstein. The pale ray of the moon fell upon his dark features, and his coruscating eye fixed on his trembling victim's countenance, flashed with almost intolerable brilliancy. A chill horror darted through Wolfstein's sickening frame; his brain swam around wildly, and most appalling presentiments of what was about to happen, pressed upon his agonized intellect. "Yes, yes, I have promised, and I will perform the covenant I have entered into," said Wolfstein; "I swear to you that I will!" and as he spoke, a kind of mechanical and inspired feeling steeled his soul to fortitude; it seemed to arise independently of himself; nor could he, though he eagerly desired to do so, control, in the least, his own resolves. Such an impulse as this had first induced him to promise at all. Ah! how often in Ginotti's absence had he resisted it! but when the mysterious disposer of the events of his existence was before him, a consciousness of the inutility of his refusal compelled him to submit to the mandates of a being, whom his heart sickening to acknowledge, it unwillingly confessed as a superior.

"Come," continued Ginotti; "the hour is late, I must dispatch."

Unresisting, yet speaking not, Wolfstein conducted Ginotti to an apartment.

"Bring wine, and light a fire," said he to the servant, who quickly obeyed him. Wolfstein swallowed an overflowing goblet, hoping thereby to acquire courage; for he found that, with every moment of Ginotti's stay, the visionary and awful terrors of his mind augmented.

"Do you not drink?"

"No," replied Ginotti, sullenly.

A pause ensured; during which the eyes of Ginotti, glaring with demoniacal scintillations, spoke tenfold terrors to the soul of Wolfstein. He knitted his brows and bit his lips, in vain attempting to appear unembarrassed. "Wolfstein!" at last said Ginotti, breaking the fearful silence; "Wolfstein!"

The colour fled from the cheek of his victim, as thus Ginotti spoke: he moved his posture, and awaited, in anxious and horrible solicitude, the declaration which was, as he supposed, to ensue. "My name, my family, and the circumstances which have attended my career through existence, it neither boots you to know, nor me to declare."

"Does it not?" said Wolfstein, scarcely knowing what to say; yet convinced, from the pause, that something was expected.

"No! nor canst thou, nor any other existing being, even attempt to dive into the mysteries which envelope me. Let it be sufficient for you to know, that every event in your life has not only been known to me, but has occurred under my particular machinations."

Wolfstein started. The terror which had blanched his cheek now gave way to an expression of fierceness and surprise; he was about to speak, but Ginotti, noticing not his motion, thus continued:

"Every opening idea which has marked, in so decided and so eccentric an outline, the fiat of your future destiny, has not been unknown to or unnoticed by me. I rejoiced to see in you, whilst young, the progress of that genius which in mature time would entitle you to the reward which I destine for you, and for you alone. Even when far, far away, when the ocean perhaps has roared between us, have I known your thoughts, Wolfstein; yet have I known them neither by conjecture nor inspiration. Never would your mind have attained that degree of expansion or excellence had not I watched over its every movement, and taught the sentiment, as it unfolded itself, to despise contented vulgarity. For this, and for an event far more important than any your existence yet has been subjected to, have I watched over you: say, Wolfstein, have I watched in vain?"

Each feeling of resentment vanished from Wolfstein's bosom, as the mysterious intruder spoke: his voice at last died, in a clear and melancholy cadence, away; and his expressive eye, divested of its fierceness and mystery, rested on Wolfstein's countenance with a mild benignity.

"No, no; thou hast not watched in vain, mysterious disposer of my existence. Speak! I burn with curiosity and solicitude to learn for what thou hast thus superintended me:" and as thus he spoke, a feeling of resistless anxiety to know what would be the conclusion of the night's adventure, took place of horror. Inquiringly he gazed on the countenance of Ginotti, the features of whom were brightened with unwonted animation. "Wolfstein," said Ginotti, "often hast thou sworn that I should rest in the grave in peace:—now listen."

# VII

*If Satan had never fallen.*
*Hell had been made for thee.*

—The Revenge

Ah! poor, unsuspecting innocence! and is that fair flower about to perish in the blasts of dereliction and unkindness? Demon indeed must he be who could gaze on those mildly-beaming eyes, on that perfect form, the emblem of sensibility, and yet plunge the spotless mind of which it was an index, into a sea of repentance and unavailing sorrow. I should scarce suppose even a demon would act so, were there not many with hearts more depraved even than those of fiends, who first have torn some unsophisticated soul from the pinnacle of excellence, on which it sat smiling, and then triumphed in their hellish victory when it writhed in agonized remorse, and strove to hide its unavailing regret in the dust from which the fabric of her virtues had arisen. "Ah! I fear me, the unsuspecting girl will go;" she knows not the malice and the wiles of perjured man—and she is gone!

It was late in the evening, and Eloise had returned from her mother's funeral, sad and melancholy; yet even amidst the oppression of grief, surprise and astonishment, pleasure and thankfulness, that any one should notice her, possessed her mind as she read over and over the characters traced on the note which she still held in her hand. The hour was late; the moon was down, yet countless stars bedecked the almost boundless hemisphere. The mild beams of Hesper slept on the glassy surface of the lake, as, scarcely agitated by the zephyr of evening, its waves rolled in slow succession; the solemn umbrage of the pine-trees, mingled with the poplar, threw their undefined shadows on the water; and the nightingale, sitting solitary in the hawthorn, poured on the listening stillness of evening, her grateful lay of melancholy. Hark! her full strains swell on the silence of night, and now they die away, with lengthened and solemn cadence, insensibly into the breeze, which lingers, with protracted sweep, along the valley. Ah! with what enthusiastic ecstacy of melancholy does he whose friend, whose dear friend, is far, far away, listen to such strains as these! perhaps he has heard them with that friend,—with one he loves: never again may they meet his ear. Alas! 't is melancholy; I even now see him sitting on the rock which looks over the lake, in frenzied listlessness; and counting in mournful review, the days which are past since they fled so quickly with one who was dear to him.

It was to the ruined abbey which stood on the southern side of the lake that, so swiftly, Eloise is hastening. A presentiment of awe filled her mind; she gazed, in inquiring terror, around her, and scarce could persuade herself that shapeless forms lurked not in the gloomy recesses of the scenery.

She gained the abbey; in melancholy fallen grandeur its vast ruins reared their pointed casements to the sky. Masses of disjointed stone were scattered around; and, save by the whirrings of the bats, the stillness which reigned, was uninterrupted. Here then was Eloise to meet the strange one who professed himself to be her friend. Alas! poor Eloise believed him. It yet wanted an hour to the time of appointment; the expiration of that hour Eloise awaited. The abbey brought to her recollection a similar ruin which stood near St. Irvyne; it brought with it the remembrance of a song which Marianne had composed soon after her brother's death. She sang, though in a low voice:

### SONG

*How stern are the woes of the desolate mourner.*

*As he bends in still grief o'er the hallowed bier.*
*As enanguish'd he turns from the laugh of the scorner.*
*And drops, to perfection's remembrance, a tear;*
*When floods of despair down his pale cheek are streaming.*
*When no blissful hope on his bosom is beaming.*
*Or, if lull'd for a while, soon he starts from his dreaming.*
*And finds torn the soft ties to affection so dear.*
*Ah! when shall day dawn on the night of the grave.*
*Or summer succeed to the winter of death?*
*Rest awhile, hapless victim, and Heaven will save*
*The spirit, that faded away with the breath.*
*Eteruity points in its amaranth bower.*
*Where no clouds of fate o'er the sweet prospect lower.*
*Unspeakable pleasure, of goodness the dower.*
*When woe fades away like the mist of the heath.*

She ceased: the melancholy cadence of her angelic voice died in faint reverberations of echo away, and once again reigned stillness.

Now fast approached the hour; and, ere ten had struck, a stranger of towering and gigantic proportions walked along the ruined refectory; without stopping to notice other objects, he advanced swiftly to Eloise, who sat on a mishapen piece of ruin, and, throwing aside the mantle which enveloped his figure, discovered to her astonished sight the stranger of the Alps, who of late had been incessantly present to her mind. Amazement, for a time, chained each faculty in stupefaction; she would have started from her seat, but the stranger, with gentle violence grasping her hand, compelled her to remain where she was.

"Eloise," said the stranger, in a voice of the most fascinating tenderness—"Eloise!"

The softness of his accents changed, in an instant, what was passing in the bosom of Eloise. She felt no surprise that he knew her name; she experienced no dread at this mysterious meeting with a person, at the bare mention of whose name she was wont to tremble: no, the ideas which filled her mind were indefinable. She gazed upon his countenance for a moment, then, hiding her face in her hands, sobbed loudly.

"What afflicts you, Eloise?" said the stranger: "how cruel, that such a breast as thine should be tortured by pain!"

"Ah!" cried Eloise, forgetting that she spoke to a stranger; "how can one avoid sorrow, when there, perhaps, is scarce a being in the world whom I can call my friend; when there is no one on whom I lay claim for protection?"

"Say not, Eloise," cried the stranger, reproachfully, yet benignly; "say not that you can claim none as a friend—you may claim me. Ah! that I had ten thousand existences, that each might be devoted to the service of one whom I love more than myself! Make me then the repository of your every sorrow and secret. I love you, indeed I do, Eloise, and why will you doubt me?"

"I do not doubt you, stranger," replied the unsuspecting girl; "why should I doubt you? for you could have no interest in saying so, if you did not.—I thank you for loving one who is quite, quite friendless; and, if you will allow me to be your friend, I will love you too. I never loved any one, before, but my poor mother and Marianne. Will you then, if you are a friend to me, come and live with me and Marianne, at St. Irvyne's?"

"St. Irvyne's!" exclaimed the stranger, almost convulsively, as he interrupted her; then, as fearing to betray his emotions, he paused, yet quitted not the grasp of Eloise's hand, which trembled within his with feelings which her mind distrusted not.

"Yes, sweet Eloise, I love you indeed." At last he said, affectionately, "And I thank you much for believing me; but I cannot live with you at St. Irvyne's. Farewell, for to-night, however; for my poor Eloise has need of sleep." He then was quitting the abbey, when Eloise stopped him to inquire his name.

"Frederic de Nempere."

"Ah! then I shall recollect Frederio de Nempere, as the name of a friend, even if I never again behold him."

"Indeed I am not faithless; soon shall I see you again. Farewell, beloved Eloise." Thus saying, with rapid step he quitted the ruin.

Though he was now gone, the sound of his tender farewell yet seemed to linger on the ear of Eloise; but with each moment of his absence, became lessened the conviction of his friendship, and heightened the suspicions which, though unaccountable to herself, possessed her bosom. She could not conceive what motive could have led her to own her love for one whom she feared, and felt a secret terror, from the conviction of the resistless empire which he possessed within her: yet though she shrank from the bare idea of ever becoming his, did she ardently, though scarcely would she own it to herself, desire again to see him.

Eloise now returned to Geneva: she resigned herself to sleep, but even in her dreams was the image of Nempere present to her imagination. Ah! poor deluded Eloise, didst thou think a man would merit thy love through disinterestedness? didst thou think that one who supposed himself superior, yet inferior in reality, to you, in the scale of existent beings, would desire thy society from love? yet superior as the fool here supposes himself to be to the creature whom he injures, superior as he boasts himself, he may howl with the fiends of darkness, in never-ending misery, whilst thou shalt receive, at the throne of the God whom thou hast loved, the rewards of that unsuspecting excellence, which he who boasts his superiority, shall suffer for trampling upon. Reflect on this, ye libertines, and, in the full career of the lasciviousness which has unfitted your souls for enjoying the slightest real happiness here or hereafter, tremble! Tremble! I say; for the day of retribution will arrive. But the poor Eloise need not tremble; the victims of your detested cunning need not fear that day: no!—then will the cause of the broken-hearted be avenged, by Him to whom their wrongs cry for redress.

Within a few miles of Geneva, Nempere possessed a country-house: thither did he persuade Eloise to go with him; "For," said he, "though I cannot come to St. Irvyne's, yet my friend will live with me."

"Yes indeed I will," replied Eloise; for whatever she might feel when he was absent, in his presence she felt insensibly softened, and a sentiment nearly approaching to love would, at intervals, take possession of her soul. Yet was it by no means an easy task to lure Eloise from the paths of virtue; it is true she knew but little, nor was the expansion of her mind such as might justify the exultations of a fiend at a triumph over her virtue; yet was it that very timid, simple innocence, which prevented Eloise from understanding to what the deep-laid sophistry of her false friend tended; and, not understanding it, she could not be influenced by its arguments. Besides, the principles and morals of Eloise were such, as could not easily be shaken by the allurements which temptation might throw out to her unsophisticated innocence.

"Why," said Nempere, "are we taught to believe that the union of two who love each other is wicked, unless authorized by certain rites and ceremonials, which certainly cannot change the tenour of sentiments which it is destined that these two people should entertain of each other?"

"It is, I suppose," answered Eloise calmly, "because God has willed it so; besides," continued she, blushing at she knew not what, "it would—"

"And is then the superior and towering soul of Eloise subjected to sentiments and prejudices so stale and vulgar as these?" interrupted Nempere indignantly. "Say, Eloise, do not you think it an insult to two souls, united to each other in the irrefragable covenants of love and congeniality; to promise, in the sight of a Being whom they know not, that fidelity which is certain otherwise?"

"But I do know that Being!" cried Eloise with warmth; "and when I cease to know him, may I die! I pray to him every morning, and, when I kneel at night, I thank him for the mercy which he has shown to a poor friendless girl like me! He is the protector of the friendless, and I love and adore him!"

"Unkind Eloise! how canst thou call thyself friendless? Surely, the adoration of two beings unfettered by restraint, must be most acceptable!—But, come, Eloise, this conversation is nothing to the purpose: I see we both think alike, although the terms in which we express our sentiments are different. Will you sing to me, dear Eloise?"

Willingly did Eloise fetch her harp; she wished not to scrutinize what was passing in her mind, but, after a short prelude, thus began:

## SONG

### I

*Ah! faint are her limbs, and her footstep is weary.*
*Yet far must the desolate wanderer roam;*
*Though the tempest is stern, and the mountain is dreary.*
*She must quit at deep midnight her pitiless home.*
*I see her swift foot dash the dew from the whortle.*
*As she rapidly hastes to the green grove of myrtle;*
*And I hear, as she wraps round her figure the kirtle.*
*"Stay thy boat on the lake,—dearest Henry, I come."*

### II

*High swell'd in her bosom the throb of affection.*
*As lightly her form bounded over the lea.*
*And arose in her mind every dear recollection:*
*"I come, dearest Henry, and wait but for thee."*
*How sad, when dear hope every sorrow is soothing.*
*When sympathy's swell the soft bosom is moving.*
*And the mind the mild joys of affection is proving.*
*Is the stern voice of fate that bids happiness flee!*

### III

*Oh! dark lower'd the clouds' on that horrible eve.*
*And the moon dimly gleam'd through the tempested air;*
*Oh! how could fond visions such softness deceive?*
*Oh! how could false hope rend a bosom so fair?*
*Thy love's pallid corse the wild surges are laving.*
*O'er his form the fierce swell of the tempest is raving;*
*But, fear not, parting spirit; thy goodness is saving.*
*In eternity's bowers, a seat for thee there.*

"How soft is that strain!" cried Nempere, as she concluded.

"Ah!" said Eloise, sighing deeply; "It is a melancholy song; my poor brother wrote it, I remember, about ten days before he died. 'Tis a gloomy tale concerning him; he ill deserved the fate he met. Some future time I will tell it you; but now, 'tis very late.—Good-night."

Time passed, and Nempere, finding that he must proceed more warily, attempted no more to impose upon the understanding of Eloise by such palpably baseless arguments; yet, so great and so unaccountable an influence had he gained on her unsuspecting soul, that ere long, on the altar of vice, pride, and malice, was immolated the innocence of the spotless Eloise. Ah, ye proud! in the severe consciousness of unblemished reputation, in the fallacious opinion of the world, why turned ye away, as if fearful of contamination, when yon poor frail one drew near? See the tears which steal adown her cheek!—She has repented, ye have not!

And thinkest thou, libertine, from a principle of depravity—thinkest thou that thou hast raised thyself to the level of Eloise, by trying to sink her to thine own?—No!—Hopest thou that thy curse has passed away unheeded or unseen? The God whom thou hast insulted has marked thee!—In the everlasting tablets of heaven, is thine offence written!—but poor Eloise's crime is obliterated by the mercy of Him, who knows the innocence of her heart.

Yes—thy sophistry hath prevailed, Nempere!—'t is but blackening the memoir of thine offences!—Hark! what shriek broke upon the enthusiastic silence of twilight?—'T was the fancied scream of one who loved Eloise long ago, but now is—dead. It warns thee—alas! 't is unavailing!!—'T is fled, but not for ever.

It is evening; the moon, which rode in cloudless and unsullied majesty, in the leaden-coloured east, hath hidden her pale beams in a dusky cloud, as if blushing to contemplate a scene of so much wickedness.

'T is done; and amidst the vows of a transitory delirium of pleasure, regret, horror, and misery, arise! they shake their Gorgon locks at Eloise! appalled she shudders with affright, and shrinks from the contemplation of the consequences of her imprudence. Beware, Eloise!—a precipice, a frightful precipice yawns at thy feet! advance yet a step further, and thou perishest!—No, give not up thy religion—it is that alone which can support thee under the miseries, with which imprudence has so darkly marked the progress of thine existence!

# VIII

*The elements respect their Maker's seal!*
*Still like the scathed pine-tree's height.*
*Braving the tempests of the night.*
*Have I' scap'd the bickering flame.*
*Like the scath'd pine, which a monument stands*
*Of faded grandeur, which the brands*
*Of the tempest-shaken air*
*Have riven on the desolate heath;*
*Yet it stands majestic even in death.*
*And rears its wild from there.*

—Wandering Jew

Yet, in an attitude of attention, Wolfstein was fixed, and, gazing upon Ginotti's countenance, awaited his narrative.

"Wolfstein," said Ginotti, "the circumstances which I am about to communicate to you are, many of them, you may think, trivial; but I must be minute, and, however the recital may excite your astonishment, suffer me to proceed without interruption."

Wolfstein bowed affirmatively—Ginotti thus proceeded:

"From my earliest youth, before it was quenched by complete satiation, curiosity, and a desire of unveiling the latent mysteries of nature, was the passion by which all the other emotions of my mind were intellectually organized. This desire first led me to cultivate, and with success, the various branches of learning which led to the gates of wisdom. I then applied myself to the cultivation of philosophy, and the éclât with which I pursued it, exceeded my most sanguine expectations. Love I cared not for; and wondered why men perversely sought to ally themselves with weakness. Natural philosophy at last became the peculiar science to which I directed my eager inquiries; thence was I led into a train of labyrinthic meditations. I thought of death—I shuddered when I reflected, and shrank in horror from the idea, selfish and self-interested as I was, of entering a new existence to which I was a stranger. I must either dive into the recesses of futurity, or I must not, I cannot die.—'Will not this nature—will not the matter of which it is composed, exist to all eternity? Ah! I know it will; and, by the exertions of the energies with which nature has gifted me, well I know it shall.' This was my opinion at that time: I then believed that there existed no God. Ah! at what an exorbitant price have I bought the conviction that there is one!!! Believing that priestcraft and superstition were all the religion which man ever practised, it could not be supposed that I thought there existed supernatural beings of any kind. I believed nature to be self-sufficient and excelling; I supposed not, therefore, that there could be any thing beyond nature.

"I was now about seventeen: I had dived into the depths of metaphysical calculations. With sophistical arguments had I convinced myself of the non-existence of a First Cause, and, by every combined modification of the essences of matter, had I apparently proved that no existences could possibly be, unseen by human vision. I had lived, hitherto, completely for myself; I cared not for others; and, had the hand of fate swept from the list of the living every one of my youthful associates, I should have remained immoved and fearless. I had not a friend in the world;—I cared for nothing but self. Being fond of calculating the effects of poison, I essayed one, which I had composed, upon a youth who had offended me; he lingered a month, and then expired in agonies the most terrific. It was returning from his funeral, which all the students of the college where I received my education (Salamanca), had attended, that a train of the strangest thought pressed upon my mind. I feared, more than ever, now, to die; and, although I had no right to form hopes or expectations for longer life than is allotted to the rest of mortals, yet did I think it were possible to protract existence. And why, reasoned I with myself, relapsing into melancholy, why am I to suppose that these muscles or fibres are made of stuff more durable than those of other men? I have no right to suppose otherwise than that, at the end of the time allotted by nature, for the existence of the atoms which compose my being, I must, like all other men, perish, perhaps everlastingly.— Here in the bitterness of my heart, I cursed that nature and chance which I believed in; and, in a paroxysmal frenzy of contending passions, cast myself, in desperation, at the foot of a lofty ash-tree, which reared its fantastic form over a torrent which dashed below.

"It was midnight; far had I wandered from Salamanca; the passions which agitated my brain, almost to delirium, had added strength to my nerves, and swiftness to my feet; but after many hours' incessant walking, I began to feel fatigued. No moon was up, nor did one star illume the hemisphere. The sky was veiled by a thick covering of clouds;

and, to my heated imagination, the winds, which in stern cadence swept along the night-scene, whistled tidings of death and annihilation. I gazed on the torrent, foaming beneath my feet; it could scarcely be distinguished through the thickness of the gloom, save at intervals, when the white-crested waves dashed at the base of the bank on which I stood. 'T was then that I contemplated self-destruction; I had almost plunged into the tide of death, had rushed upon the unknown regions of eternity, when the soft sound of a bell from a neighbouring convent, was wafted in the stillness of the night. It struck a chord in unison with my soul; it vibrated on the secret springs of rapture. I thought no more of suicide, but, reseating myself at the root of the ash-tree, burst into a flood of tears;—never had I wept before; the sensation was new to me; it was inexplicably pleasing. I reflected by what rules of science I could account for it: there philosophy failed me. I acknowledged its inefficacy; and, almost at that instant, allowed the existence of a superior and beneficent Spirit, in whose image is made the soul of man; but quickly chasing these ideas, and, overcome by excessive and unwonted fatigue of mind and body, I laid my head upon a jutting projection of the tree, and, forgetful of every thing around me, sank into a profound and quiet slumber. Quiet, did I say? No—It was not quiet. I dreamed that I stood on the brink of a most terrific precipice, far, far above the clouds, amid whose dark forms which lowered beneath, was seen the dashing of a stupendous cataract: its roarings were borne to mine ear by the blast of night. Above me rose, fearfully embattled and rugged, fragments of enormous rocks, tinged by the dimly gleaming moon; their loftiness, the grandeur of their mishapen proportions, and their bulk, staggering the imagination; and scarcely could the mind itself scale the vast loftiness of their aerial summits. I saw the dark clouds pass by, borne by the impetuosity of the blast, yet felt no wind myself. Methought darkly gleaming forms rode on their almost palpable prominences.

"Whilst thus I stood, gazing on the expansive gulf which yawned before me, methought a silver sound stole on the quietude of night. The moon became as bright as polished silver, and each star sparkled with scintillations of inexpressible whiteness. Pleasing images stole imperceptibly upon my senses, when a ravishingly sweet strain of dulcet melody seemed to float around. Now it was wafted nearer, and now it died away in tones to melancholy dear. Whilst I thus stood enraptured, louder swelled the strain of seraphic harmony; it vibrated on my inmost soul, and a mysterious softness lulled each impetuous passion to repose.

I gazed in eager anticipation of curiosity on the scene before me; for a mist of silver radiance rendered every object but myself imperceptible; yet was it brilliant as the noon-day sun. Suddenly, whilst yet the full strain swelled along the empyrean sky, the mist in one place seemed to dispart, and, through it, to roll clouds of deepest crimson. Above them, and seemingly reclining on the viewless air, was a form of most exact and superior symmetry. Rays of brilliancy, surpassing expression, fell from his burning eye, and the emanations from his countenance tinted the transparent clouds below with silver light. The phantasm advanced towards me; it seemed then, to my imagination, that his figure was borne on the sweet strain of music which filled the circumambient air. In a voice which was fascination itself, the being addressed me, saying, 'Wilt thou come with me? wilt thou be mine?' I felt a decided wish never to be his. 'No, no,' I unhesitatingly cried, with a feeling which no language can either explain or describe. No sooner had I uttered these words than methought a sensation of deadly horror chilled my sickening frame; an earthquake rocked the precipice beneath my feet; the beautiful being vanished; clouds, as of chaos, rolled around, and from their dark masses flashed incessant meteors. I heard a deafening noise on every side; it appeared like the dissolution of nature; the blood-red moon, whirled from her sphere, sank beneath the horizon. My neck was grasped firmly, and, turning round in an agony of horror, I beheld a form more hideous than the imagination of man is capable of portraying, whose proportions, gigantic and deformed, were seemingly blackened by the inerasible traces of the thunderbolts of God; yet in its hideous and detestable countenance, though seemingly far different, I thought I could recognise that of the lovely vision: 'Wretch!' it exclaimed, in a voice of exulting thunder; 'saidst thou that thou wouldst not be mine? Ah! thou art mine beyond redemption; and I triumph in the conviction, that no power can ever make thee otherwise. Say, art thou willing to be mine?' Saying this, he dragged me to the brink of the precipice: the contemplation of approaching death frenzied my brain to the highest pitch of horror. 'Yes, yes, I am thine,' I exclaimed. No sooner had I pronounced these words, than the visionary scene vanished, and I awoke. But even when awake, the contemplation of what I had suffered, whilst under the influence of sleep, pressed upon my disordered fancy; my intellect, wild with unconquerable emotions, could fix on no one particular point to exert its energies; they were strained beyond their power of exerting.

PERCY BYSSHE SHELLEY

"Ever, from that day, did a deep-corroding melancholy usurp the throne of my soul. At last during the course of my philosophical inquiries, I ascertained the method by which man might exist for ever, and it was connected with my dream. It would unfold a tale of too much horror to trace, in review, the circumstances as then they occurred; suffice it to say, that I became acquainted that a superior being really exists: and ah! how dear a price have I paid for the knowledge! To one man, alone, Wolfstein, may I communicate this secret of immortal life: then must I forego my claim to it,—and oh! with what pleasure shall I forego it! To you I bequeath the secret; but first you must swear that if—you wish God may—"

"I swear," cried Wolfstein, in a transport of delight; burning ecstacy revelled through his veins; pleasurable coruscations were emitted from his eyes. "I swear," continued he; "and if ever—may God—" "Needless were it for me," continued Ginotti, "to expatiate further upon the means which I have used to become master over your every action; that will be sufficiently explained when you have followed my directions. Take," continued Ginotti, "—and—and—mix them according to the directions which this book will communicate to you. Seek, at midnight, the ruined abbey near the castle of St. Irvyne, in France; and there—I need say no more—there you will meet with me."

# IX

The varying occurrences of time and change, which bring anticipation of better days, brought none to the hapless Eloise. Nempere now having gained the point which his villany had projected, felt little or no attachment left for the unhappy victim of his baseness; he treated her indeed most cruelly, and his unkindness added greatly to the severity of her afflictions. One day, when, weighed down by the extreme asperity of her woes, Eloise sat leaning her head on her hand, and mentally retracing, in sickening and mournful review, the concatenated occurrences which had led her to become what she was, she sought to change the bent of her ideas, but in vain. The feelings of her soul were but exacerbated by the attempt to quell them. Her dear brother's death, that brother so tenderly beloved, added a sting to her sensations. Was there any one on earth to whom she was now attracted by a wish of pouring in the friend's bosom ideas and feelings indefinable to any one else? Ah, no! that friend existed not; never, never more would she know such a friend. Never did she really love any one; and now had she sacrificed her conviction of right and wrong to a man who neither knew how to appreciate her excellence, nor was adequate to excite other sensation than of terror and dread.

Thus were her thoughts engaged, when Nempere entered the apartment, accompanied by a gentleman, whom he unceremoniously announced as the Chevalier Mountfort, an Englishman of rank, and his friend. He was a man of handsome countenance and engaging manners. He conversed with Eloise with an ill-disguised conviction of his own superiority, and seemed indeed to assert, as it were, a right of conversing with her; nor did Nempere appear to dispute his apparent assumption. The conversation turned upon music; Mountfort asked Eloise her opinion; "Oh!" said Eloise, enthusiastically, "I think it sublimes the soul to heaven; I think it is, of all earthly pleasures, the most excessive. Who, when listening to harmoniously-arranged sounds of music, exists there, but must forget his woes, and lose the memory of every earthly existence in the ecstatic emotions which it excites? Do you not think so, Chevalier?" said she; for the liveliness of his manner enchanted Eloise, whose temper, naturally elastic and sprightly, had been damped as yet by misery and seclusion. Mountfort smiled at the energetic avowal of her feelings; for, whilst she yet spoke, her expressive countenance became irradiated by the emanation of sentiment.

"Yes," said Mountfort, "it is indeed powerfully efficient to excite the interests of the soul; but does it not, by the very act of resuscitating the feelings, by working upon theperhaps, long dead chords of secret and enthusiastic rapture, awaken the powers of grief as well as pleasure?"

"Ah! it may do both," said Eloise, sighing.

He approached her at that instant. Nempere arose, as if intentionally, and left the room. Mountfort pressed her hand to his heart with earnestness: he kissed it, and then resigning it, said, "No, no, spotless untainted Eloise; untainted even by surrounding depravity:—not for worlds would I injure you. Oh! I can conceal it no longer—will conceal it no longer—Nempere is a villain."

"Is he?" said Eloise, apparently resigned, now, to the severest shocks of fortune: "then, then indeed I know not with whom to seek an asylum. Methinks all are villains."

"Listen then, injured innocence, and reflect in whom thou hast confided. Ten days ago, in the gaming-house at Geneva, Nempere was present. He engaged in play with me, and I won of him considerable sums. He told me that he could not pay me now, but that he had a beautiful girl whom he would give to me, if I would release him from the obligation. 'Est elle une fille de joye?' I inquired. 'Oui, et de vertu practicable.' This quieted my conscience. In a moment of licentiousness, I acceded to his proposal; and, as money is almost valueless to me, I tore the bond for three thousand zechins: but did I think that an angel was to be sacrificed to the degrading avarice of the being to whom her fate was committed? By heavens, I will this moment seek him,—upbraid him with his inhuman depravity,—and—" "Oh! stop, stop," cried Eloise, "do not seek him; all, all is well—I will leave him. Oh! how I thank you, stranger, for this unmerited pity to a wretch who is, alas! too conscious that she deserves it not."—"Ah! you deserve every thing," interrupted the impassioned Mountfort; "you deserve paradise. But leave this perjured villain; and do not say, unkind fair-one, that you have no friend; indeed you have a most warm, disinterested friend in me."—"Ah! but," said Eloise, hesitatingly, "what will the—"

"World say," she was about to have added; but the conviction of having so lately and so flagrantly violated every regard to its opinion— she only sighed. "Well," continued Mountfort, as if not perceiving her hesitation; "you will accompany me to a cottage ornée which I possess at some little distance hence? Believe that your situation shall be treated with the deference which it requires; and, however I may have yielded to habitual licentiousness, I have too much honour to disturb the sorrows of one who is a victim to that of another." Licentious and free as had been the career of Mountfort's life, it was by no means the result of a nature naturally prone to vice; it had been owing to the unchecked sallies of an imagination not sufficiently refined. At the desolate situation of Eloise, however, every good propensity in his nature urged him to take compassion on her. His heart, originally susceptible of the finest feelings, was touched, and he really and sincerely—yes, a libertine, but not one from principle, sincerely meant what he said.

"Thanks, generous stranger," said Eloise, with energy; "indeed I do thank you." For not yet had acquaintance with the world sufficiently bidden Eloise distrust the motives of its disciples. "I accept your offer, and only hope that my compliance may not induce you to regard me otherwise than I am."

"Never, never can I regard you as other than a suffering angel," replied the impassioned Mountfort. Eloise blushed at what the energetic force of Mountfort's manner assured her was not intended as a compliment.

"But may I ask my generous benefactor, how, where, and when am I to be released?"

"Leave that to me," returned Mountfort: "be ready to-morrow night at ten o'clock. A chaise will wait beneath."

Nempere soon entered; their conversation was uninterrupted, and the evening passed away uninteresting and slow.

Swiftly fled the intervening hours, and fast advanced the moment when Eloise was about to try, again, the compassion of the world. Night came, and Eloise entered the chaise; Mountfort leaped in after her. For a while her agitation was excessive. Mountfort at last succeeded in calming her; "Why, my dearest Ma'am'selle" said he, "why will you thus needlessly agitate yourself? I swear to hold your honour far dearer than my own life; and my companion—"

"What companion?" Eloise interrupted him, inquiringly.

"Why," replied he, "a friend of mine, who lives in my cottage; he is an Irishman, and so very moral, and so averse to every species of gaieté de coeur, that you need be under no apprehensions. In short, he is a love-sick swain, without ever having found what he calls a congenial female. He wanders about, writes poetry, and, in short, is much too sentimental to occasion you any alarm on that account. And, I assure you," added he, assuming a more serious tone, "although I may not be quite so far gone in romance, yet I have feelings of honour and humanity which teach me to respect your sorrows as my own."

"Indeed, indeed I believe you, generous stranger; nor do I think that you could have a friend whose principles are dishonourable."

Whilst yet she spoke, the chaise stopped, and Mountfort, springing from it, handed Eloise into his habitation. It was neatly fitted up in the English taste.

"Fitzeustace," said Mountfort to his friend, "allow me to introduce you to Madame Eloise de—." Eloise blushed, as did Fitzeustace.

"Come," said Fitzeustace, to conquer mauvaise honte, "supper is ready, and the lady doubtlessly fatigued."

Fitzeustace was finely formed, yet there was a languor which pervaded even his whole figure; his eyes were dark and expressive, and as, occasionally, they met those of Eloise, gleamed with excessive brilliancy, awakened doubtlessly by curiosity and interest. He said but little during supper, and left to his more vivacious friend the whole of Eloise's conversation, who animated at having escaped a persecutor, and one she hated, displayed extreme command of social powers. Yes, once again was Eloise vivacious: the sweet spirit of social intercourse was not dead within,—that spirit which illumes even slavery, which makes its horrors less terrific, and is not annihilated in the dungeon itself.

At last arrived the hour of retiring—Morning came.

The cottage was situated in a beautiful valley. The odorous perfume of roses and jasmine wafted on the zephyr's wing, the flowery steep which rose before it, and the umbrageous loveliness of the surrounding country, rendered it a spot the most fitted for joyous seclusion. Eloise wandered out with Mountfort and his friend to view it; and so accommodating was her spirit, that, ere long, Fitzeustace became known to her as familiarly as if they had been acquainted all their lives.

Time fled on, and each day seemed only to succeed the other purposely to vary the pleasures of this delightful retreat. Eloise sung in the summer evenings, and Fitzeustace, whose taste for music was most exquisite, accompanied her on his oboe.

By degrees the society of Fitzeustace, to which before she had preferred Mountfort's, began to be more interesting. He insensibly acquired a power over the heart of Eloise, which she herself was not aware of. She involuntarily almost sought his society; and when, which frequently happened, Mountfort was absent at Geneva, her sensations were indescribably ecstatic in the society of his friend. She sat in mute, in silent rapture, listening to the notes of his oboe, as they floated on the stillness of evening: she feared not for the future, but, as it were, in a dream of rapturous delight, supposed that she must ever be as now—happy; not reflecting that, were he who caused that happiness absent, it would exist no longer.

Fitzeustace madly, passionately doted on Eloise: in all the energy of incontaminated nature, he sought but the happiness of the object of his whole affections. He sought not to investigate the causes of his woe; sufficient was it for him to have found one who could understand, could sympathize in, the feelings and sensations which every child of nature whom the world's refinements and luxury have not vitiated, must feel,—that affection, that contempt of selfish gratification, which every one whose soul towers at all above the multitude, must acknowledge. He destined Eloise, in his secret soul, for his own. He resolved to die—he wished to live with her; and would have purchased one instant's happiness for her with ages of hopeless torments to be inflicted on himself. He loved her with passionate and excessive tenderness: were he absent from her but a moment, he would sigh with love's impatience for her return; yet he feared to avow his flame, lest this, perhaps, baseless dream of rapturous and enthusiastic happiness might fade;—then, indeed Fitzeustace felt that he must die.

Yet was Fitzeustace mistaken: Eloise loved him with all the tenderness of innocence; she confided in him unreservedly; and, though unconscious of the nature of the love she felt for him, returned each enthusiastically energetic prepossession of his towering mind with ardour excessive and unrestrained. Yet did Fitzeustace suppose that she loved him not. Ah! why did he think so?

Late one evening, Mountfort had gone to Geneva, and Fitzeustace wandered with Eloise towards that spot which Eloise selected as their constant evening ramble on account of its superior beauty. The tall ash and oak, in mingled umbrage, sighed far above their heads; beneath them were walks, artificially cut, yet imitating nature. They wandered on, till they came to a pavilion which Mountfort had caused to be erected. It was situated on a piece of land entirely surrounded by water, yet peninsulated by a rustic bridge which joined it to the walk.

Hither, urged mechanically, for their thoughts were otherwise employed, wandered Eloise and Fitzeustace. Before them hung the moon in cloudless majesty; her orb was reflected by every movement of the crystalline water, which, agitated by the gentle zephyr, rolled tranquilly. Heedless yet of the beauties of nature, the loveliness of the scene, they entered the pavilion.

Eloise convulsively pressed her hand on her forehead.

"What is the matter, my dearest Eloise?" inquired Fitzeustace, whom awakened tenderness had thrown off his guard.

"Oh! nothing, nothing; but a momentary faintness. It will soon go off; let us sit down."

They entered the pavilion.

"'Tis nothing but drowsiness," said Eloise, affecting gaiety; "'t will soon go off. I sate up late last night; that I believe was the occasion."

"Recline on this sofa, then," said Fitzeustace, reaching another pillow to make the couch easier; "and I will play some of those Irish tunes which you admire so much."

Eloise reclined on the sofa, and Fitzeustace, seated on the floor, began to play; the melancholy plaintiveness of his music touched Eloise; she sighed, and concealed her tears in her handkerchief. At length she sunk into a profound sleep: still Fitzeustace continued playing, noticing not that she slumbered. He now perceived that she spoke, but in so low a tone, that he knew she slept.

He approached. She lay wrapped in sleep; a sweet and celestial smile played upon her countenance, and irradiated her features with a tenfold expression of etheriality. Suddenly the visions of her slumbers appeared to have changed; the smile yet remained, but its expression was melancholy; tears stole gently from under her eyelids:—she sighed.

Ah! with what eagerness of ecstacy did Fitzeustace lean over her form! He dared not speak, he dared not move; but pressing a ringlet of hair which had escaped its band, to his lips, waited silently.

"Yes, yes; I think—it may—" at last she muttered; but so confusedly, as scarcely to be distinguishable.

Fitzeustace remained rooted in rapturous attention, listening.

"I thought, I thought he looked as if he could love me," scarcely articulated the sleeping Eloise. "Perhaps, though he may not love me, he may allow me to love him.—Fitzeustace!"

On a sudden, again were changed the visions of her slumbers; terrified she started from sleep, and cried, "Fitzeustace!"

# X

*For love is heaven, and heaven is love.*

—Lay of the last Minstrel

Needless were it to expatiate on their transports; they loved each other, and that is enough for those who have felt like Eloise and Fitzeustace.

One night, rather later indeed than it was Mountfort's custom to return from Geneva, Eloise and Fitzeustace sat awaiting his arrival. At last it was too late any longer even to expect him; and Eloise was about to bid Fitzeustace good-night, when a knock at the door aroused them. Instantly, with a hurried and disordered step, his clothes stained with blood, his countenance convulsed and pallid as death, in rushed Mountfort.

An involuntary exclamation of surprise burst from the terrified Eloise.

"What—what is the matter?"

"Oh, nothing, nothing!" answered Mountfort, in a tone of hurried, yet desperate agony. The wildness of his looks contradicted his assertions. Fitzeustace, who had been inquiring whether he was wounded, on finding that he was not, flew to Eloise.

"Oh! go, go!" she exclaimed. "Something, I am convinced, is wrong.— Tell me, dear Mountfort, what it is—in pity tell me."

"Nempere is dead!" replied Mountfort, in a voice of deliberate desperation; then, pausing for an instant, he added in an under tone, "And the officers of justice are in pursuit of me. Adieu, Eloise!— Adieu, Fitzeustace! You know I must part with you—you know how unwillingly.—My address is at—London.—Adieu—once again adieu!"

Saying this, as by a convulsive effort of despairing energy, he darted from the apartment, and mounting a horse which stood at the gate, swiftly sped away. Fitzeustace well knew the impossibility of his longer stay; he did not seem surprised, but sighed.

"Ah! well I know," said Eloise, violently agitated, "I well know myself to be the occasion of these misfortunes. Nempere sought for me; the generous Mountfort would not give me up, and now is he compelled to fly—perhaps may not even escape with life. Ah! I fear it is destined that

PERCY BYSSHE SHELLEY

every friend must suffer in the fatality which environs me. Fitzeustace!" she uttered this with such tenderness, that, almost involuntarily, he clasped her hand, and pressed it to his bosom, in the silent, yet expressive enthusiasm of love. "Fitzeustace! you will not likewise desert the poor isolated Eloise?"

"Say not isolated, dearest love. Can, can you fear, my love, whilst your Fitzeustace exists? Say, adored Eloise, shall we now be united, never, never to part again? Say, will you consent to our immediate union?"

"Know you not," exclaimed Eloise, in a low, faltering voice, "know you not that I have been another's?

"Oh! suppose me not," interrupted the impassioned Fitzeustace, "the slave of such vulgar and narrow-minded prejudice. Does the frightful vice and ingratitude of Nempere sully the spotless excellence of my Eloise's soul?—No, no,—that must ever continue uncontaminated by the frailty of the body in which it is enshrined. It must rise superior to the earth: 't is that which I adore, Eloise. Say, say, was that Nempere's?"

"Oh! no, never!" cried Eloise, with energy. "Nothing but fear was Nempere's."

"Then why say you that ever you were his?" said Fitzeustace, reproachfully. "You never could have been his, destined as you were for mine, from the first instant the particles composing the soul which I adore, were assimilated by the God whom I worship."

"Indeed, believe me, dearest Fitzeustace, I love you, far beyond any thing existing—indeed, existence were valueless, unless enjoyed with you!"

Eloise, though a something prevented her from avowing them, felt the enthusiastic and sanguine ideas of Fitzeustace to be true: her soul, susceptible of the most exalted virtue and expansion, though cruelly nipped in its growth, thrilled with delight unexperienced before, when she found a being who could understand and perceive the truth of her feelings, and indeed anticipate them, as did Fitzeustace; and he, while gazing on the index of that soul, which associated with his, and animated the body of Eloise, but for him, felt delight, which, glowing and enthusiastic as had been his picture of happiness, he never expected to know. His dark and beautiful eye gleamed with tenfold luster; his every nerve, his every pulse, confessed the awakened consciousness, that she, on whom his soul had doted, ever since he acknowledged the existence of his intellectuality, was present before him.

A short space of time passed, and Eloise gave birth to the son of Nempere. Fitzeustace cherished it with the affection of a father, and, when occasionally he necessarily must be absent from the apartment of his beloved Eloise, his whole delight was to gaze on the child, and trace in its innocent countenance the features of the mother who was so beloved by him.

Time no longer dragged heavily to Eloise and Fitzeustace: happy in the society of each other, they wished nor wanted other joys; united by the laws of their God, and assimilated by congeniality of sentiment, they supposed that each succeeding month must be like this, must pass like this in the full satiety of every innocent union of mental enjoyment. While thus the time sped in rapturous succession of delight, autumn advanced.

The evening was late, when, at the usual hour, Eloise and Fitzeustace took the way to their beloved pavilion. Fitzeustace was unusually desponding, and his ideas for futurity were marked by the melancholy of his mind. Eloise in vai, attempted to soothe him; the contention of his mind was but too visible. She led him to the pavilion. They entered it. The autumnal moon had risen; her dimly-gleaming orb, scarcely now visible, was shrouded in the duskiness of the atmosphere: like a spirit of the spotless ether, which shrinks from the obtrusive gaze of man, she hung behind a leaden-coloured cloud. The wind in low and melancholy whispering sighed among the branches of the towering trees; the melody of the nightingale, which floated upon its dying cadences, alone broke on the solemnity of the scene. Lives there, whose soul experiences no degree of delight, is susceptible of no gradations of feelings, at change of scenery? Lives there, who can listen to the cadence of the evenign zephyr, and not acknowledge, in his mind, the sensations of celestial melancholy which it awakens? for if he does, his life were valueless, his death were undeplored. Ambition, avarice, ten thousand mean, ignoble passions, had extinguished within him that soft, but indefinable sensorium of unallayed delight, with which his soul, whose susceptibility is not destroyed by the demands of selfish appetite, thrills exultingly, and wants but the union of another, of whom the feelings are in unison with his own, to constitute almost insupportable delight.

Let Epicureans argue, and say, "There is no pleasure but in the gratification of the senses." Let them enjoy their own opinion; I want not pleasure, when I can enjoy happiness. Let Stoics say, "Every idea that there are fine feelings, is weak; he who yields to them is even weaker." Let those too, wise in their own conceit, indulge themselves in sordid and degrading hypotheses; let them suppose human nature capable of no influence from anything but materiality; so long as I enjoy the innocent and congenial delight, which it were needless to define to those who are strangers to it, I am satisfied.

"Dear Fitzeustace," said Eloise, "tell me what afflicts you; why are you so melancholy?—Do not we mutually love, and have we not the unrestrained enjoyment of each other's society?"

Fitzeustace sighed deeply; he pressed Eloise's hand. "Why does my dearest Eloise suppose that I am unhappy?" The tone of his voice was tremulous, and a deadly settled paleness dwelt on his cheek.

"Are you not unhappy, then, Fitzeustace?"

"I know I ought not to be so," he replied, with a faint smile;—he paused—"Eloise," continued Fitzeustace, "I know I ought not to grieve, but you will, perhaps, pardon me when I say, that a father's curse, whether from the prejudice of education, or the innate consciousness of its horror, agitates my mind. I cannot leave you, I cannot go to England; and will you then leave your country, Eloise, to accommodate me? No, I do not, I ought not to expect it."

"Oh! with pleasure; what is country? what is every thing without you? Come, my love, dismiss these fears, we yet may be happy."

"But before we go to England, before my father will see us, it is necessary that we should be married—nay, do not start, Eloise; I view it in the light that you do; I consider it an human institution, and incapable of furnishing that bond of union by which alone can intellect be conjoined; I regard it as but a chain, which, although it keeps the body bound, still leaves the soul unfettered: it is not so with love. But still, Eloise, to those who think like us, it is at all events harmless; 't is but yielding to the prejudices of the world wherein we live, and procuring moral expediency, at a slight sacrifice of what we conceive to be right.

"Well, well, it shall be done, Fitzeustace," resumed Eloise; "but take the assurance of my promise that I cannot love you more."

They soon agreed on a point of, in their eyes, so trifling importance, and arriving in England, tasted that happiness, which love and innocence alone can give. Prejudice may triumph for a while, but virtue will be eventually the conqueror.

# Conclusion

I t was night—all was still; not a breeze dared to move, not a sound to break the stillness of horror. Wolfstein has arrived at the village near which St. Irvyne stood; he has sped him to the château, and has entered the edifice; the garden door was open, and he entered the vaults.

For a time, the novelty of his situation, and the painful recurrence of past events, which, independently of his own energies, would gleam upon his soul, rendered him too much confused to investigate minutely the recesses of the cavern. Arousing himself, at last, however, from this momentary suspension of faculty, he paced the vaults in eager desire for the arrival of midnight. How inexpressible was his horror when he fell on a body which appeared motionless and without life! He raised it in his arms, and, taking it to the light, beheld, pallid in death, the features of Megalena. The laugh of anguish which had convulsed her expiring frame, still played around her mouth, as a smile of horror and despair; her hair was loose and wild, seemingly gathered in knots by the convulsive grasp of dissolution. She moved not; his soul was nerved by almost superhuman powers; yet the ice of despair chilled his burning brain. Curiosity, resistless curiosity, even in a moment such as this, reigned in his bosom. The body of Megalena was breathless, and yet no visible cause could be assigned for her death. Wolfstein dashed the body convulsively on the earth, and, wildered by the suscitated energies of his soul almost to madness, rushed into the vaults.

Not yet had the bell announced the hour of midnight. Wolfstein sate on a projecting mass of stone; his frame trembled with a burning anticipation of what was about to occur; a thirst of knowledge scorched his soul to madness; yet he stilled his wild energies,—yet he awaited in silence the coming of Ginotti. At last the bell struck; Ginotti came; his step was rapid, and his manner wild; his figure was wasted almost to a skeleton, yet it retained its loftiness and grandeur; still from his eye emanated that indefinable expression which ever made Wolfstein shrink appalled. His cheek was sunken and hollow, yet was it flushed by the hectic of despairing exertion. "Wolfstein," he said, "Wolfstein, part is past—the hour of agonizing horror is past; yet the dark and icy gloom of desperation braces this soul to fortitude;—but come, let us to business." He spoke, and threw his mantle on the ground. "I am blasted to endless torment," muttered the mysterious. "Wolfstein, dost thou deny thy Creator?"—"Never, never."—"Wilt thou not?"—"No, no,—any thing but that."

Deeper grew the gloom of the cavern. Darkness almost visible seemed to press around them; yet did the scintillations which flashed from Ginotti's burning gaze, dance on its bosom. Suddenly a flash of lightning hissed through the lengthened vaults: a burst of frightful thunder seemed to convulse the universal fabric of nature; and, borne on the pinions of hell's sulphurous whirlwind, he himself, the frightful prince of terror, stood before them. "Yes," howled a voice superior to the bursting thunderpeal; "yes, thou shalt have eternal life, Ginotti." On a sudden Ginotti's frame mouldered to a gigantic skeleton, yet two pale and ghastly flames glared in his eyeless sockets. Blackened in terrible convulsions, Wolfstein expired; over him had the power of hell no influence. Yes, endless existence is thine, Ginotti—a dateless and hopeless eternity of horror.

Ginotti is Nempere. Eloise is the sister of Wolfstein. Let then the memory of these victims to hell and malice live in the remembrance of those who can pity the wanderings of error; let remorse and repentance expiate the offences which arise from the delusion of the passions, and let endless life be sought from Him who alone can give an eternity of happiness.

THE END

# A Note About the Author

Percy Bysshe Shelley (1792–1822) was an English Romantic poet. Born into a prominent political family, Shelley enjoyed a quiet and happy childhood in West Sussex, developing a passion for nature and literature at a young age. He struggled in school, however, and was known by his colleagues at Eton College and University College, Oxford as an outsider and eccentric who spent more time acquainting himself with radical politics and the occult than with the requirements of academia. During his time at Oxford, he began his literary career in earnest, publishing *Original Poetry by Victor and Cazire* (1810) and *St. Irvyne; Or, The Rosicrucian: A Romance* (1811). In 1811, he married Harriet Westbrook, with whom he lived an itinerant lifestyle while pursuing affairs with other women. Through the poet Robert Southey, he fell under the influence of political philosopher William Godwin, whose daughter Mary soon fell in love with the precocious young poet. In the summer of 1814, Shelley eloped to France with Mary and her stepsister Claire Claremont, travelling to Holland, Germany, and Switzerland before returning to England in the fall. Desperately broke, Shelley struggled to provide for Mary through several pregnancies while balancing his financial obligations to Godwin, Harriet, and his own father. In 1816, Percy and Mary accepted an invitation to join Claremont and Lord Byron in Europe, spending a summer in Switzerland at a house on Lake Geneva. In 1818, following several years of unhappy life in England, the Shelleys—now married—moved to Italy, where Percy worked on *The Masque of Anarchy* (1819), *Prometheus Unbound* (1820), and *Adonais* (1821), now considered some of his most important works. In July of 1822, Shelley set sail on the *Don Juan* and was lost in a storm only hours later. His death at the age of 29 was met with despair and contempt throughout England and Europe, and he is now considered a leading poet and radical thinker of the Romantic era.

# A Note from the Publisher

Spanning many genres, from non-fiction essays to literature classics to children's books and lyric poetry, Mint Edition books showcase the master works of our time in a modern new package. The text is freshly typeset, is clean and easy to read, and features a new note about the author in each volume. Many books also include exclusive new introductory material. Every book boasts a striking new cover, which makes it as appropriate for collecting as it is for gift giving. Mint Edition books are only printed when a reader orders them, so natural resources are not wasted. We're proud that our books are never manufactured in excess and exist only in the exact quantity they need to be read and enjoyed.

# Discover more of your favorite classics with Bookfinity™.

- Track your reading with custom book lists.
- Get great book recommendations for your personalized Reader Type.
- Add reviews for your favorite books.
- AND MUCH MORE!

Visit **bookfinity.com** and take the fun Reader Type quiz to get started.

Enjoy our classic and modern companion pairings!

www.ingramcontent.com/pod-product-compliance
Lightning Source LLC
Chambersburg PA
CBHW020543130626
46552CB00007B/2737